SAPPHIC SPARKS

Vol. 1

NATALIE NAUDUS

MARY HELEN GALLUCCI

Little Mountain Media

ISBN 979-8-9900801-3-3 (Trade paperback)

Cover art by Nienke Slotbloom
IG: @becauseofmyloveforwomen
www.myloveforwomen.nl

Cover design by Mary Helen Gallucci

*To all the women for whom
lusting after a woman
is sacred*

Sparks

Spark Synopses vii
Introduction xi

1. CHERRY ON TOP 1
by Mary Helen Gallucci

2. FOX SPIRIT 19
by Natalie Naudus

3. ON THE EDGE 37
by Natalie Naudus and Mary Helen Gallucci

4. MOTHER SUPERIOR 49
by Mary Helen Gallucci

5. COZY MORNING 65
by Mary Helen Gallucci

6. YES, CAPTAIN 73
by Natalie Naudus

7. TWO OF CUPS 83
by Mary Helen Gallucci

8. THE DUET 101
by Natalie Naudus

9. PRICK OF HER TEETH 113
by Natalie Naudus and Mary Helen Gallucci

10. YARN & YEARNING 123
by Mary Helen Gallucci

11. LOVE ME TENDER 149
by Natalie Naudus and Mary Helen Gallucci

12. ROADSIDE ASSISTANCE 159
by Natalie Naudus

13. MOLAMELONS 169
by Mary Helen Gallucci

14. HOME FOR CHRISTMAS   181
by Natalie Naudus

15. ICE TIME   193
by Natalie Naudus

16. THE ART OF SOUP   203
by Mary Helen Gallucci

Acknowledgments   219
About the Authors   221
Find Us Online!   223

Spark Synopses

Cherry on Top
1

Based on Natalie's viral video about a queer-coded bakery next to a tattoo shop: two neighboring business owners hit it off after hours in the pantry. Hidden tattoos may be found . . . ingredients may be contaminated.

Fox Spirit
19

What if a multi-tailed fox spirit—the East Asian equivalent of a succubus—was sapphic? What if the pleasure shared between women could be a source of magical strength? In this beautiful, gentle mythological reimagining, a princess runs away with her faithful (and secretly supernatural) bodyguard . . .

On the Edge
37

Britt thinks Lianne's romance novel is just absurdly unrealistic, because of *course* nobody can come on demand. Lianne's determination to prove her girlfriend wrong goes from playful . . . to desperate.

Mother Superior
49

There's a rebellious new nun at the abbey, and she is just begging for punishment. Against all her better judgment, Mother Veronica might have to give it to her . . .

Cozy Morning
65

No plot, just a whole lot of stream-of-conscious morning lady-wood.

Yes, Captain
73

The captain of a starship has a public disagreement with her chief science officer. Later, they meet to work out their differences.

Two of Cups
83

Brooke's roommate, Jenna, is her best friend, but she'd do anything to be more. Anything *but* stack the tarot deck when Jenna asks her for a reading . . . right?

The Duet
101

Beth and Chris are happily married, and happily polyamorous. When Beth meets up with a much younger woman, she discovers they have something unexpected in common.

The Prick of Her Teeth
113

This girl Clarissa's been seeing has it all: she's witty, gorgeous, well-traveled, and has an amazing house. But Lilith only seems more mysterious as they spend more time together. Could there be more to her than meets the eye?

Yarn & Yearning
123

Two short, neurodivergent girls in a craft store vs. one crucial ball of lesbian-colored yarn in a very high basket. One car running on empty in a snow-storm vs. one distracting audiobook sex scene, and an even more distracting girl in the passenger seat. What could possibly go wrong?

Love Me Tender
149

Helena has big plans for her partner's cozy domestic celebration, just the two of them. But her body has other plans, and she's not sure she can physically pull it off . . . Her pain may be chronic but their night won't be platonic!

ROADSIDE ASSISTANCE
159

A flat tire is ruining Andi's day . . . until a very attractive handywoman shows up to offer her services. This woman has got to be good with more than just car mechanics, and Andi is dying to find out.

MOLAMELONS
169

Uvalia and Syd have almost nothing in common: their species share a planet and not much else. But after a lucky, sticky rescue at the market one morning, they realize big differences can be fascinating . . .

HOME FOR CHRISTMAS
181

Missing your wife while she's long distance is hard, and single parenting is exhausting. But parting makes the reunion afterward all the sweeter . . .

ICE TIME
193

When the hockey coach gets into a fight with the figure skating coach, they take to the rink (and the locker room) to resolve their differences. Could their heated argument melt the ice between them?

THE ART OF SOUP
203

Astrid is secretly thrilled when Sora's stealth attack disrupts her excruciatingly mundane stake-out. She's got the upper hand, and soon Sora is tied up in the cellar, at her mercy. But why won't Sora break? What is her secret?

Introduction

Hi! Thanks for picking up our book! We hope you find something that warms you, something that makes you feel seen . . . and maybe even a sense of sapphic community, here in these pages.

In a book of fictional love and lust stories, here's one that's true.

Natalie

Mary Helen and I met on Zoom. She was cute and shy, a newer audiobook narrator who scheduled a few coaching sessions with me. I found her charming and smart. We talked shop: best audiobook practices, website, samples, how to get work. We met a few more times, and I helped her hone a few samples and auditions. I had this sense that we had a lot in common, or at least that there was a lot that I'd like to know about her. But I'm really conscious of people's time in their sessions, so I kept things as professional and informative as I could.

Somehow, despite both of us being quite reserved and introverted, we started chatting outside of Zoom, and we fell hard and fast into friendship. And wow was I right, we did have a lot in common. We'd both come out to ourselves in our thirties, having spent our lives until then in various homophobic denominations of Christianity. We'd both studied music in college. My husband and Mary Helen had both been music education majors and school teachers from the Midwest. I admired her incredible courage, having quit her job at a Catholic school that was crushing her whole soul, and starting up a new career while parenting her kids with a contentious ex. I couldn't help but love her. But I was monogamous and happily married, and I had no idea how to begin talking to my husband about what this all meant. I wasn't sure, myself, what was happening. So we kept talking, as friends—but my feelings were growing.

Mary Helen

Those first few Zooms with Natalie were unforgettable. I'd had to voice a horse in a passage we were working on, and when she had to turn away from the camera to laugh into her elbow at my whinny . . . I'm not sure anything had ever felt better. I could not *for the life of me* put on a British accent in her presence—my brain just flew out my ear. I found I was blushing so profusely for so long after one session that I concluded it must have been sunburn. I iced my face with a bag of frozen peas.

Natalie was so encouraging and so kind, I was astounded over and over at how she managed to land constructive criticism so gently that it never even pinched. We're just both such sensitive souls—and so used to both receiving and giving private music lessons—it was like we spoke the same language from the start. She felt immediately safe; I'd never experienced anything like it. I've never met anyone like her.

When I landed my first narration gig with a publisher—thanks in part to networking and a glowing recommendation from Natalie—I felt the acute need to send her a thank you card to express my gratitude. But despite visiting every card shop in my city, I could not find a card that captured the vibe I wanted: light but sincere, effusive and heartfelt but also gay and fun, soft and cute but also—y'know—professional? Reader, I could not find one single card that accomplished this, so by the end of the day I had bought no fewer than 72 imperfect cards. Eventually I chose one and just added a rainbow of exclamation points all over the front of it with fine-tipped markers. I later learned that Natalie's husband, Don, had immediately seen it for the love letter it was, though that had truly not been my conscious intention.

Natalie

That September, I was on vacation and driving with my husband and kids through Indiana. I texted Mary Helen, "Driving past your town, waving to you!" I had mentioned that we were going to be passing through her area, but wasn't sure if she wanted to meet up with all four of us, knowing that she's quite introverted. She texted me back, and we pulled off the highway to meet at a beach on the shore of Lake Michigan. I still remember walking out to the shore, the light impossibly bright on the water, and there she was: beautiful, hair blowing gently in the breeze, one hand holding a plastic bucket and shovel for my kids to play in the sand, her other hand in the back pocket of her shorts.

It's weird having forbidden feelings. I kept them so hidden that I didn't acknowledge them even to myself. But looking back now, I know that I hoped meeting her would cement her as a friend in my mind. I hoped I wouldn't find her beautiful. I hoped seeing her in person would dim her allure. But she was beautiful, and kind to my kids. She chatted with Don about music education conferences and growing up in the Midwest, and my heart was swelling further with impossible, impossible feelings.

Mary Helen

My experience meeting Natalie on the beach was so similar: I too had sincerely hoped she'd seem somehow flawed in real life, so I could move on with my feelings. But instead, the opposite happened. It was surreal walking across the sand and spotting her, sun glinting off her dark braid, face so gentle and radiant as she played with her children. I fixated on my sandals for most of the couple of hours we spent together, because I was so afraid I'd stare at her, otherwise. Afraid she or Don would clock my feelings for what they were.

I still have mental snapshots of the way her lips moved over her teeth, the way her purse strap laid across the giraffe on her t-shirt, the then-fresh tattoo on her arm, and the way we accidentally stared into each other's souls for one truly electric moment. She put such clear effort into connecting with me and making me comfortable, and yet I was completely tongue-tied—it was so much easier to talk with Don! At one point Natalie asked if I played the piano, and I just said, "Yes." I was sure she'd never want to speak to me again.

Natalie

On the contrary, we talked even more after that meeting, texting daily about queerness, parenting, and our evolving feelings about God. I finished a draft of my novel which would become *Gay the Pray Away*, and she read it and validated my feelings so persuasively that I thought, maybe I won't hide this story forever. Maybe it's worth sharing with others.

Maybe this was how we flirted? I've never really known how to flirt, and I wasn't trying to fall in love—I was bonding with a soul. We talked a lot about how confusing friendship had been as queer women: how often we've looked back and thought, was I in love with that friend? Or were we platonic soul sisters? How could we tell the difference?

Mary Helen

As we were bonding so deeply over her book, and working together to disentangle our religious trauma and sexual identities, I could see Natalie unfurling into her most beautiful, confident, queer self: it was beyond inspiring to witness. But along the way, as she came to know me, my history, and my insecurities, she promised that she'd be my friend forever . . . and that tore me up. Because I wanted that more than anything, but I knew the intensity of my feelings for her. I knew I would have to let her go if I couldn't navigate them without hurting her and/or her husband. I knew she fully loved him, and that even if I had the power, in no fantasy would I ever wish the (all-too-familiar) pain of divorce and split custody on *anyone,* much less the person I was coming to treasure most in the world. But something felt so deeply *right* between us, and I felt so sure we understood each other, that this desire not to hurt either of them just deepened my determination to figure out how to navigate all those feelings. I had to hope it was possible.

Eventually, my therapist told me it was time to address things directly. I was terrified I'd lose Natalie's friendship, but the truth was that I didn't think I could see her again for an upcoming audiobook conference and contain myself without breaking my own heart. I had to choose between pre-emptively canceling and generating some distance, or taking the very real risk of communicating my feelings.

Natalie

Mary Helen texted me, saying that she needed to talk to me about something. Then she said very plainly, "I'm in love with you. I know you are monogamous and married, but is there any chance you'd talk to Don about it, and love me back?"

What followed was a lot of talking. With Don, with Mary Helen—each of us speaking to therapists, alone and as couples. It wasn't easy or simple, and eventually I'll take the time to write about all of it . . . but writing this today, life is so beautiful. I've been with Mary Helen for two years, still happily married to Don. Our kids are great friends and we get together as often as we can. And I've been given the greatest gift. The chance to love a woman with my one precious life, and to have her love me.

I've recorded over five hundred audiobooks, and I'd estimate a good three hundred of those are romances—many of them sapphic. Being active in online sapphic book spaces, a common request I see is: what's the spiciest book I can pick up? There are so many fantastic sapphic (and spicy!) romances these days, but we hope this collection of short stories helps to fill that niche for anyone looking for concentrated sapphic "sparks": heartfelt, loving, passionate stories about women desiring each other and finding fulfillment, written with care by us, for us.

Writing these stories together has been such a labor of love. We brainstorm ideas together, check in with each other while writing, sometimes trade back and forth to get a story to completion. Because of unavoidable differences in location, it's been lovely to have an ongoing artistic endeavor together. After I record the story, Mary Helen edits and masters it prior to posting it monthly on our Sapphic Sparks Patreon. A million thank yous to our patrons who have kept us going, helped support our big poly family, and given us feedback on a new story each month!

SAPPHIC SPARKS

ONE

Cherry on Top

by Mary Helen Gallucci

*J*eri strode into Ava's bakery late one afternoon, as Ava was pulling the day's unsold baked goods from her display. "Hey, some guy has been crying in my bathroom over there for like an hour—do you mind if I use yours a minute? I really gotta pee."

Sunlight was streaming warmly through the windows, set high in the far wall, and catching Jeri's dark hair so it glowed a rich chocolate. Ava caught herself staring. "Of course! Want some day-olds, while you're here?" She extended a tray with a smattering of cookies, and thrilled privately when the other woman slowed and drew closer, coming to lean against the counter to consider her choice.

In nearly a year of owning her bakery, Ava had scarcely had an excuse to talk to Jeri. For one thing, their work hours didn't overlap much: Ava had to be up well before the crack of dawn, usually preheating her ovens by 3:45 each morning, while the doors to Jeri's tattoo parlor didn't open until 10. Jeri was only ever a brief vision, there and gone again, during Ava's busiest hours. So, as reluctant as Ava usually was to socialize, she was not going to miss this opportunity to finally interact with the gorgeous artist next door.

Jeri hummed as she selected an almond-studded bar.

"Oh my god, good choice—those are my grandma's recipe. They've been called 'Better than Sex Biscotti.' That was actually how I had them on the menu for a while, but some parents complained."

Jeri smirked, accepting one. The cookie was softer than true biscotti, baked just once. "Oh my god," she moaned, pausing mid-chew. Her eyes rolled for a moment, her eyelashes fluttering. "Okay, I kind of get the name."

"That was a pretty excellent face; I might . . . remember that, if you don't mind." Oh fuck, what a weird thing to say. Had Ava seriously said that out loud? And the "if you don't mind" just made it so much worse. Why *would* Jeri mind, unless she'd meant it like—

"Don't get me wrong, this is incredible . . . but did someone actually *say* it was 'better than sex?' Out loud?"

Ava felt her face flush. "It was—my ex. I don't love sharing that part." Yet she just had? *Why?* What was it about Jeri that prompted only the most awkward words to come spilling out of Ava's mouth unexamined? She could've just said *yes* and escaped the question with her pride intact. "I mean also," she quickly amended, "those have been sitting out since six o'clock this morning. They're *much* better warm."

Jeri's eyebrows rose subtly, and she looked at the cookie with . . . was that *distaste*? Then she looked back at Ava, scrutinizing. Following her eyes, Ava glanced down at the front of her apron, brushing at the flour on the maroon canvas there to no effect.

"I mean, Ava, I guess I wouldn't know, but—" was it just her, or was Jeri's voice a little huskier than it had been a moment ago? "I'm pretty skeptical."

If Ava's ex had called that cookie better than sex, was Jeri taking it all the way to . . . better than sex with *her?* Had she just been *imagining* sex with Ava? And—thinking it might be better than the cookie? That was—a ridiculous leap; Ava had to be reading way too far into this. But if that *wasn't* what she'd meant, then . . . was Jeri insulting her baking?

Ava quickly snatched one of the bars and took a bite herself. "Is there something wrong with the batch? I can't have been selling bad cookies all day and just—"

"Hey. No, the biscotti's great, it's delicious. I just meant—it's not an insult, I just meant I could *imagine* something *more* delicious. Especially if sex is on the table." Ava's eyes had a moment to widen before Jeri hastily added, "As a point of comparison."

"Oh," was all Ava could manage. Her face was burning, and she was sure Jeri could tell, which made it all the worse. It crossed her mind that she was relieved Jeri couldn't see her body's *other* reactions to this . . . comment that felt almost like a suggestion? An offer?

"Thanks for the freebie, though—I should come over here after you close more often." Jeri glanced at the door and shifted her weight off the counter, making like she was about to leave.

"I thought you had to pee?"

"Oh . . . yeah, actually that's right." And in a few strides, Jeri pushed past the swinging doors towards the kitchen.

Ava breathed a sigh of relief that the other woman seemed to know where she was headed. With that confident gait . . . she must've been in the back before? Maybe before Ava had bought the little interior shop front from the chocolatiers who had sized up and moved uptown. The bathroom was tucked away behind an unlikely narrow door in the pantry. Ava wondered if the pantry light was on. It probably wasn't. But a minute had slid by since Jeri had disappeared—maybe two—so she must have found it . . . right?

Ava envisioned Jeri in the dark pantry, feeling along the walls for the light switch with her inked fingers. Among all Jeri's tattoos, Ava had fixated on the details of these ones in her numerous, if brief, sightings of the other woman around their shops. A vine wound its way from her right forearm, across her wrist up the base of her thumb, and forked to curl around her index finger as well. A snake's delicate tail tickled her left elbow, coiling up her arm to finally lick her tapered pinky. . . . Ava imagined those fingers grazing sacks of flour, jars stacked on industrial shelves, feeling for a toggle on the wall when really, the bare bulb in the pantry had a pull chain that dangled well above Ava's head.

Ava should go in there. There was no way Jeri would have found it. Except—she was a *completely* competent woman, and if Ava was honest with herself, she wasn't certain her motives were altruistic. Did she just want, for a moment, to *be* in the dark pantry with Jeri? She inhaled sharply, seeing a flash of that snake's tongue extending not toward bags of flour, but her own—

The swinging doors swivelled aggressively behind her and Ava found herself suddenly in the kitchen, hastening toward the pantry much too fast to really process that its light was, in fact, on. Reaching it, she stopped in the middle of the small room to take stock of what she was doing there, and then registered a low voice behind her: "Hey, where's the fire?"

Ava whirled and saw Jeri, who stood with a bowl cupped in her hands. Her embellished fingers were deftly twined in the cloth cover, and she was hunched slightly over it, like she'd been sniffing its contents. "That's—" Ava stuttered, "that's the fruit I'm soaking for bourbon cake . . ."

Jeri nodded emphatically, her voice hushed with nostalgia

as she explained: "I picked out this scent on my way in; I haven't smelled this since my grandma's kitchen, when I was a kid. I think this is *exactly* the same bourbon as she used?! Hers always smelled of . . . vanilla, and honey, with the sharp tang of cherries. Just like this."

Jeri's eyes fluttered closed again as she took another long whiff, and Ava tried to skip her mind past identifying the expression as Jeri's "better than sex" face. "Did you . . . find the bathroom, then?" Ava sputtered.

Jeri's eyes opened, and now Ava felt them burning into her again. They were a honey brown; brighter than Ava had pictured. But of course, the fluorescent light was on now. "Yeah, I did," said Jeri.

"Great!" Ava wondered if she should . . . leave Jeri to her sniffing? But no—this was *her* bakery. If the onus was on someone to leave, that someone was Jeri. . . . Only, she looked very comfortable right where she was. *Very* comfortable, leaning her tanned shoulder casually against the shelving unit. Her work boots seemed pretty much rooted to the pantry's cement floor.

And the truth was, she didn't want Jeri to leave. Not even a little bit. The truth was, she'd admired the woman for years, from a safe distance. She wasn't *certain* Jeri was queer—they hadn't actually had a conversation about it, and she hadn't seen her with a partner—but her tattoo parlor certainly attracted the crowd. It sported so much Pride swag from local queer artists that the color practically leapt from the walls, along with strains of Brandi Carlisle, every time the parlor door opened. This had actually been one of the reasons Ava had overbid the listing price on her bakery the first day she'd spotted it on the market: Jeri's shop next door had looked something like home to her, even though she herself had never dared to commit to a tattoo. Yet.

Jeri was still watching her, and—it was altogether too warm. She'd been running the ovens all morning and there wasn't any ventilation in the tiny room. Ava found herself untying her apron, slinging it awkwardly over her forearm. "You can try some if you'd like," she offered.

Jeri's gaze narrowed on Ava for a moment longer. Then another. A moment *too* long. It made Ava feel for a moment as if she'd accidentally pulled off the rest of her clothes along with her apron. Finally, Jeri spoke. "Should I just . . . use my fingers?"

Ava's jaw dropped open, just a little. Those *fingers.* They were long and muscular, tan under the ink; the knuckles prominent, nails short. The way they cradled that bowl, they looked—agile, dextrous: like each fingertip knew its independent role in handling what it touched . . . Ava was dying to know how she'd use them, and the heat of the other woman's eyes melted the butterflies in her stomach into something liquid and lower . . .

Suddenly Ava jumped. "Oh my god, a spoon, obviously. Hang on." She dashed out, and was back a split second later with a beechwood spoon.

She proffered the spoon to Jeri, but instead of accepting it, the other woman just extended the bowl toward her. Ava scooped up a bobbing cherry, her hand shaking slightly, and raised it to Jeri's parted lips. They looked *so* soft and perfect, her plump upper lip so delicious—Ava was mortified to hear a sigh escape her own mouth as Jeri accepted the cherry into hers, clasping it in her perfect teeth.

Jeri had definitely heard her sigh too, and Ava thought she might have seen a flicker of what looked like genuine warmth cross the other woman's face—but then Jeri's attention was on the cherry as she chewed it slowly, clearly savoring it. "Mmmmm," she purred after swallowing. "Thank you. That was amazing."

"Scale of 1 to 10 where sex is 5, where's that cherry? Better than sex?" Ava was trying for a teasing tone, but was honestly not sure she was achieving it.

"How is sex *five*?" Jeri laughed.

"It's just a *scale*!" Ava tried to roll her eyes, but her voice was coming out a bit frantic and she knew it. "These things are meaningless if you don't establish your reference points, everyone knows that!"

"I mean, sure, but you clearly need a better reference point for that one."

"Okay . . ." Ava felt a little dizzy. She set the spoon on a shelf and took the bowl from Jeri, tucking it back in its place and straightening its cloth.

"Okay?" Was Ava imagining it or did Jeri shift her weight a little closer? No—she definitely was leaning into her elbow, now, on the shelf inches from Ava's busy hands. Ava could hear her breathing. Was it heavier than usual, or were her own senses just going haywire?

Ava met her eyes. "Yeah, can—can I kiss you?"

Jeri's breath *definitely* hitched. She reached for Ava, deftly tucking a strand of hair behind her ear and then cradling her jaw in her smoothly calloused palm. "Yeah," she said. "Please." Her thumb with its delicate inked fern brushed over Ava's lips and it was so *warm* and she was so close and finally Ava lifted herself on her toes and pressed her lips to Jeri's.

For a moment, time stood still. Ava forgot to breathe, and all that mattered in the world was Jeri's soft lower lip against her own.

And then—everything was moving. Jeri tangled her hands in Ava's hair and pulled her closer, turning so that she was pressing Ava's back to the plywood column supporting the shelves. Jeri kissed her with what felt like desperation, but couldn't be—the woman had such composure and also such *fire* and Ava felt herself melting, dizzy with the awareness that this was *her*, this was *Jeri*, and fuck but she was real and solid and moving under Ava's hands, kissing her and nipping at her lip like Jeri *wanted* her. Like she'd eaten her cookie and her cherry and was still just so hungry for more. Better.

Ava ran the tip of her tongue over Jeri's upper lip, and the other woman gasped—had she forgotten to breathe too?—and Ava savored the taste of her. She was sweet, and sour — vanilla, and butterscotch, oak . . . that cherry. She tasted like an old fashioned, and something all of her own. Something that made Ava's chest swell and flutter; made her knees weak; made her all too aware that her hips were rocking, pressing her greedily against Jeri's thigh.

Ava found her hands at Jeri's waist, and pulled at the ribbed tank there, slipping her fingers under it to caress the silky expanse of Jeri's back. She grazed her fingertips up over the band of Jeri's bra, and then raked her short nails back down. Her skin was so soft, and warm, and the muscles of her back flexed under Ava's touch. Ava felt the other woman shudder, and she broke their kiss to gulp some air, tipping her face toward the ceiling and exhaling, "Is this okay?"

Jeri took the opening to devour Ava's throat, kissing and licking her pulse, moving to the hinge of her jaw and then nipping and sucking at her earlobe with a low "Mmmhm."

The fluorescent lightbulb multiplied into a starry sky as Ava squeezed her eyes shut, then popped them back open when she felt Jeri's fingers edging under the scooped neck of her top. "May I?" Jeri murmured.

"Y-yes," Ava managed, "Fuck yes."

Without hesitation, Jeri pulled down on the fabric of Ava's shirt and bra together, freeing her breast with the help of her other hand so that Ava was suddenly aware of the warm pantry air on her nipple, the skin around it glowing translucent in the bright light, in contrast to the rest of her late-summer tan.

"Holy fucking hell." Jeri's tone sounded almost—reverent, and her eyes looked hazy for the moment she met Ava's with evident effort, before dipping her head and taking Ava's nipple into her mouth.

Ava let out a yelp at the sudden heat and sensation of it, and Jeri groaned her satisfaction, rolling the tip of her tongue around Ava's nipple and then sucking it against the roof of her mouth. Ava had to brace her hands on the shelves behind her as Jeri pressed her face into the supple flesh of her breast, released Ava's nipple to lick the skin below it, palmed it and squeezed.

"Don't fucking stop," Ava whimpered, and Jeri grinned hungrily as she stretched the shirt down to release Ava's other breast. She took that one in her teeth, and when she looked up, Ava remembered how she'd taken the cherry just minutes before. Chewed it, and swallowed it . . . Jeri's teeth sank into her nipple. Ava heard herself cry out, even as her panties flooded with a mortifying surge that she was certain she felt seeping through her leggings, probably into the denim covering Jeri's thigh. She had never been this wet in her life, never seen anything as gorgeous and absolutely electric as the heat in Jeri's eyes as she bit into Ava's sensitive flesh.

Ava's hips rolled desperately against Jeri's leg until it slipped away, replaced by her palm cupping between Ava's thighs. "Oh my *god*," Jeri groaned, feeling the damp material, and then pressing the heel of her hand more firmly as Ava ground helplessly against her. Jeri's biceps bulged from the counter-pressure she was offering, and Ava might have been floating.

"Jeri—*please* touch me," Ava begged. She grabbed the other woman's hand from between her legs, registering a flash of the vine on Jeri's forefinger as Ava guided it under the bands of her clothing. She widened her stance, giving Jeri's fingers access as they combed down through her curls until the tip of one parted her and dipped in—

"So *slick*," Jeri gasped. And then she was stroking up to Ava's clit, and circling with her fingertip so effortlessly and sliding back to drench more fingers. Ava held Jeri close, breathing hotly into her neck, and she moved with Jeri's hand, pressing for more until finally she felt one long finger curl slowly inside her.

"Ffffuck, Ava, you feel incredible," Jeri murmured. She slid her finger partway out and Ava felt immediately empty and desperate before two fingers pushed back in and slid home, scissoring inside her. Ava bore down on Jeri's fingers, squeezing for more pressure. Jeri leaned in to nip at her neck, and then whispered hot in her ear: "God, you're so beautiful and so wet, I feel like I could just—play here all day."

"You are—completely welcome to," Ava said between gasps. "I obviously—want you."

"I am sincerely honored." Jeri's other hand slid down the back of Ava's thigh, gently pulling her knee up onto a shelf to spread her further.

Ava huffed a laugh as Jeri slowly pumped her fingers, adding a third, curling them to rake against her inner walls. "Yeah you—should be," she managed.

Jeri kissed her. Their mouths twined and Ava caught Jeri's bottom lip between her teeth, pulling it as she rode Jeri's fingers, the heel of Jeri's palm grinding against her needy clit —and then she released her lip to suck in a breath as pleasure started to build and swell at her core. Straining against the material of Ava's leggings, Jeri's strong hand plunged insistently into her and a low cry emerged from Ava's throat as she came undone, her muscles undulating around Jeri's fingers.

When she finally gasped again, her eyes blinked open to see Jeri, lips parted, staring at her face with an expression that mixed thrill and wonder. "Please," Jeri said, "Do *not* try to tell me the cookie wins."

Ava wished she was the kind of person who could play coy, but she knew beyond a doubt that her own face had already told the whole truth. "Okay," she panted, as the oxygen made its way back to her brain and she registered that the gorgeous woman in front of her was there, ripe, ready for her, "but I haven't even tried a taste test yet."

She surged up from where she'd been leaning and backed Jeri the few steps across the pantry until Jeri's calves hit a stack of flour sacks, and she collapsed back onto it, taking Ava with her. A faint white cloud surrounded them, and Jeri coughed a laugh. "Are we contaminating your ingredients?"

"I mean, not yet . . ." Ava grinned, then bit her lip. "Do you . . . *wanna* contaminate some ingredients?"

Now Jeri laughed in earnest. "Absolutely. I'm about to double-dip in that cherry bowl."

"Oh my god." Ava snickered. "It's my turn."

Jeri leaned up to kiss Ava again—hard, almost rough, and so distracting that Ava forgot for a moment that she had hands, and that she was hovering over a woman she'd been not-quite-shamelessly lusting after, worshiping with her eyes, for ages. Her fingers hesitated over Jeri's stomach. She was absolutely certain she wanted to explore this woman, but in her post-orgasmic haze—the banter, Jeri's heat, her breath against Ava's skin, the way Ava's own breasts hung half-exposed from her disheveled top—it felt surreal.

"I can touch you?" Ava asked. "You're sure?"

Jeri groaned. "Ava. You're killing me." She started to sit

up, crossing her arms and reaching for the hem of her tank, but Ava stopped her.

"No, wait. Please. Let me."

Jeri acquiesced. She leaned back, her elbows braced on the flour sacks, and watched Ava intently. She was just—open, available, giving Ava access, and Ava felt dizzy with the permission. Jeri there before her, *for* her, waiting to be undressed. Fuck.

Ava swallowed, exhaled shakily . . . and then began to reverently skim the ribbed material up Jeri's abdomen, over her belly button, her ribs—and she gasped. Threads of a spiderweb faded in as they rose to frame the curve just under the cup of Jeri's bra. At its center, the base of her breastbone, perched a large moth, spreading its wings. The ink was a striking black, with a realism that made the moth's furry body touchably soft, its forewings like silk. It was all layers and folds, and Ava had to edge Jeri's bra up to see better. The moth's thorax—top and center, where the wings met—looked like a glistening bead, hooded by the crest of its head.

"I designed her myself," Jeri said, as Ava brushed her thumb over the wings with wonder. Then Ava dipped her head to touch the tip of her tongue to the gleaming nub of the insect's thorax, thrilling in anticipation of doing the same to Jeri's clit. She could feel the thrum of Jeri's heartbeat against her lips, Jeri's skin so delicate and lush and delicious.

Ava's lips moved across Jeri's chest, over the material of her practical black bra which Ava unceremoniously shoved up. She kissed and sucked and nipped at Jeri's breast, and holy hell the bud of her nipple tasted so fucking good on her tongue. She needed to savor it, memorize its texture. She followed along with the other woman's movements as Jeri undulated beneath her, moaning, fisting Ava's hair, until Ava saw stars again and remembered that she had to breathe.

Panting, Ava leaned on her side next to Jeri, finally taking in the picture of her: eyes clouded, hair disheveled, her neck bent awkwardly where she propped herself back on her elbows against the cement-block wall, tank and bra rucked up, rosy nipples glistening, peaked on the gentle swells of her breasts. That spiderweb, draping down nearly to her belly button; her belted hips balanced perilously at the edge of the stack of flour bags, propped there by her feet on the floor.

God, and this was *Jeri*, the badass business owner, the artist—looking like a work of erotic art herself in *Ava's own pantry*.

"You okay?" Jeri asked her, and the gentle tone caught Ava off guard. She found herself gaping. Was intimidation all over her face? Was obsession?

"So good," Ava breathed.

"Y'know," Jeri smirked, "I saw you take a bite of one of those cookies, but you didn't look nearly this into it."

Ava choked on a laugh. "Are you insulting my baking or are you just this cocky? I wasn't *savoring* that cookie."

"Not like now."

Ava flushed. "Yeah. You're . . ."

Jeri smiled broadly, then tipped her chin up, exposing her long neck and closing her eyes. "Well. Savor away."

Ava considered denying this on principle. The other woman's nerve was a little bewildering, and she was still unclear if Jeri even . . . she found she needed to know before proceeding. "Do you actually *like* my baking?"

Jeri's eyes flew open. "Ava. Are you kidding? Why do you think I sneak over *every day* between clients for samples?"

Ava was aghast. "You do *not!*"

"I do."

"I would *absolutely* have noticed this."

Now it was Jeri's turn to look sheepish. "I'm pretty quick,

in and out. Not much of a social butterfly. I try to time it for when you're talking to other customers."

Ava squinted. "Okay, supposing this was possible—which it's not—you're saying you like my baking so much you'd . . . steal it from me while avoiding me."

"That's exactly what I'm saying, yes. I mean, it's not stealing. You offer free samples."

"To paying customers!"

"Hey, I'm a customer! I ordered my birthday cake from you this year!"

"You *did?!*"

"It would've been under my mom's name, but I told her I wanted one from you. Last May. Apricot marmalade filling, my god it was *incredible.*" Jeri's pink tongue darted out to wet her lips at the memory.

"I . . . made your birthday cake." Ava felt awash with warmth, and a little giddy at the image of her marmalade on the roof of Jeri's mouth . . . She stole a heated kiss; then she lowered herself to Jeri's belt. With trembling fingers, she pulled the end from the buckle, and yanked the prong free— the motion felt rough—and then it was open, and the button undone, and she was unzipping Jeri's jeans. The wide elastic of her waistband underneath was gray, and had letters across it, and Ava registered in that heady moment that she could *smell* Jeri, from where she knelt between her legs. Ava ran her palm over the other woman's skin, fingertips drifting over her ribs and across the edges of the spider web, and when Jeri arched her back to rise to her touch, she dipped her thumb under that wide waistband.

Jeri had to shift her weight to help shimmy the jeans off her hips; she toed off her boots and Ava helped her off with the pant legs, then dove back in. Ava rubbed her nose up and down the damp indent in the fabric between Jeri's legs, following with her thumb, and then her tongue, as Jeri whimpered and writhed. "Please, Ava, oh my god . . ."

Then Ava pulled the damp material to the side and— "Ohhh," she breathed, at the sight of Jeri's glistening folds, rosy and swollen. Maybe it was just on her mind, but Ava could've sworn she smelled like—marmalade. Syrupy-sweet and citrus, and Ava couldn't wait: she spread the folds with her fingers and slipped her tongue in.

And holy fuck the world around her disappeared and there was just —slick and warm around her tongue and soft skin against her cheeks and ears, muffling Jeri's guttural groans that Ava hardly had the space to register—this was *Jeri*, coming undone for *her*. She wrapped her arms around Jeri's thighs, pressing her face deeper as the other woman ground against her mouth and oh my god she was fucking *delicious*.

Ava let her lips slide up to Jeri's clit, sucking the nub of it to the roof of her mouth and rolling the flat of her tongue against it, savoring—*savoring*. Better than the most aromatic cookie, sweeter than powdered sugar icing as it dripped over the edge of a sponge cake—

"Ava," Jeri rasped, "Babe could you—please use your finger—"

Ava grinned up at her. "You want that spoon?"

Jeri's head dropped back as she gave a throaty laugh. Ava felt a tingling jolt of pleasure in her chest at the sound. "Just give me your fucking finger *please*, Jesus Christ I need it."

"Yes, ma'am," Ava said with delight, and acquiesced without further hesitation, wetting her forefinger along the edges of Jeri's slit, and then slipping it inside her. Jeri emitted a groan of relief. "Mmmm," Ava hummed against Jeri's clit, lapping at it with her tongue. Her finger explored and stroked the spongy ridges of Jeri's front wall, relishing the way she shook.

"God, *more*," Jeri begged, pulling her knee up toward her chest, spreading herself wide. Ava eagerly took the opening to lave broad strokes across Jeri's pussy from side to side, her mouth open wide and tongue flat as if she might devour her whole. "Another finger, please."

Ava added her middle finger, pressing in deeper, deeper until she felt the slippery bulb of the other woman's cervix. She circled it once, twice—and then Jeri was gasping "FUCK," and she was pulsing around Ava's fingers, her legs thrashing. Ava's open mouth was filled with something so wet and vaguely sweet; she sucked harder to stay with Jeri's writhing hips and not miss a delicious drop.

When Jeri finally stilled, and sagged back onto the flour sacks, Ava licked one last drip of the juices from Jeri's folds and wiped her chin on her sleeve. Then she leaned over the limp Jeri to kiss her, and the other woman returned it with fervor. Both women were panting, but Jeri's turned into a shallow chuckle.

"What?" Ava asked, cautiously.

"Come on. '*Better Than Sex* Biscotti?!' It's a joke, right?"

"Maybe it was just a ploy to bring up the topic of sex with you."

Jeri gaped at her. "*You?* Plotting against me?!"

Ava shrugged coyly. "Okay but to be fair, I didn't actually get to *see* your face just now, so we still don't know for *sure*."

Jeri chuckled, reaching for her clothes. "Oh, we don't, huh. You're telling me that was inconclusive?"

"I'm just saying, you made a *pretty great* face for that cookie. And the comparison is incomplete. But you'd better get back to work, so . . ."

Jeri paused a moment, fastening her bra. ". . . So. Same time tomorrow, is what you're asking?"

It was Ava's turn to break into laughter. "Seriously, you're going with it, just like that?"

Jeri stood to pull her jeans over her hips. "I mean unless you aren't into it . . ."

"No, I'm—*completely* on board."

Jeri smiled broadly. "Maybe if you ask nicely."

Ava stood and lifted her face to Jeri's. "Please?"

Jeri kissed her, and then again. "Mmmm . . ." She considered between kisses.

"*Pretty* please," Ava amended, "with a cherry on top?"

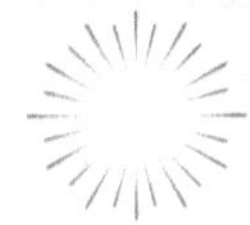

TWO

Fox Spirit

by Natalie Naudus

*I*n Chinese mythology, the many-tailed Fox Spirit is the Eastern equivalent of the Succubus: a spirit that disguises herself as a beautiful woman, and can pull energy from the souls of the men (or in this case, the woman) whom she beguiles.

I'm awakened by a sound. I sit up, reaching quickly for my sword, my ears alert in the darkness. And then I hear it again: a soft sob. Rolling out of my cot, I walk to the curtain separating me from Mei.

"My lady?" Silence. "My lady? Are you all right?"

I hear a sniffle, and she says softly, "Go back to sleep, Huli." I stand still, unsure of what to do. I can feel her distress like it's my own. Everything in me wants to go to her, to comfort her, to take her away from this place.

"Are you still there?" she whispers, soft as a falling blossom.

Pulling the curtain aside, I slip into her room. The moonlight shines gently on her face, caressing her cheek with a cool glow. Tears glimmer in her eyes, spilling down her cheeks as she looks up at me.

"Oh Huli," she cries, "I don't know what to do."

I lay my sword down, and gently, hesitatingly, put a hand on her shoulder. "My lady, I . . ."

She takes my hand in hers and presses her cheek against it. I feel the wetness of her tears, and I struggle to maintain my distance.

"Huli, please hold me. I'm sorry, I know it's not done, but we used to be so close when we were younger; you used to hold me when I was sad or scared. Please? Just this once? I need you." Her voice is quivering and her heart pulls on mine. Against my better judgment I sit on her bed, and she throws herself into my arms. Gently, I fold my arms around her. She melts into me the way she used to, sobbing quietly, and she feels so small. So frail. I wish with my entire being to protect her, to soothe away the pain, but this comfort is all I can offer.

"Shhh," I whisper as I stroke her hair. "My lady. My sweet girl."

"Remember that day we spent by the lake?" she whispers tearily.

"How could I forget?"

"We ate peaches on the bank, and when I kissed you . . ."

"You tasted so sweet," I whisper. I squeeze my eyes shut, trying to slow the powerful current of the memory. We've been close for years, Mei and I, but I know it could never be. A love between a royal lady and her guard—it's forbidden.

"I can't marry him." She pulls away and looks up at me, her eyes shining with resolve. "I won't. I won't marry him, Huli."

"What will you do?" I ask.

"Take me away. Let's flee to the mountains. We can live

with your family, up in the clouds beyond the reach of the Emperor."

"When I asked before, you said you couldn't leave." I take a slow breath, trying to calm my heart. The memory hurts. I'm afraid to hope.

"Huli, look at me." I meet her gaze. She reaches out and holds my chin gently. "I'm sorry I wasn't ready before, but do you see my resolve? I'll go with you. I'll leave everything behind and never return. Please take me with you." Her lip quivers and tears spill from her eyes. "Please take me with you. Please Huli, don't leave me here to be trapped in a love-less marriage, I need you, please," she sobs, and I hold her, her face against my chest.

I rest my cheek against her silken black hair and breathe in the scent of her. She knows me enough to trust me, but she doesn't know my deepest secret. And she deserves to know. I must tell her. I take a breath to confess, but falter. Will she still look at me with love if she knows the truth of who I am? Instead, I say, "I'll take you away from here. I promise."

For the next week, I plan with care. I don't smile at Mei when she passes me in the hall. I don't gaze at her reflection in the mirror as her handmaiden combs her hair. I don't squeeze her hand when I help her into her carriage. The path ahead of us is set, but the ease of it depends entirely on my preparation. I take fruit and nuts and dried meat from the kitchen. Worry gnaws at me about revealing the truth of my identity to her, but I steel myself to tell her at the next opportunity. I know I will need energy for the journey, so I give in to the attentions of a fellow guard and efficiently bed him to replenish my strength. And now, on the night of our departure, I carefully roll my blanket and pack it into a bag with our supplies.

. . .

When I pull back the curtain, Mei is sitting on her bed, fully dressed. She's wearing her warmest cloak, and her sturdy boots.

"Don't ask me if I'm sure." Her dark gaze is steady on mine. "I won't turn back."

I sink to my knees before her, taking her hands in mine. "There's something I must tell you. You deserve to know. I . . . my family, we . . ."

"Huli," she interrupts, tipping my chin up so gently I want to cry. "You think I haven't noticed the way you hear things no one else can? The way you can scent my time of the month and bring me warm towels and tea, or the way you know where I've been because you can sense which plants I've brushed against? Or the fact that your family lives beyond the reach of the empire, in the Cloud Mountains? You are a fox spirit."

I'm stunned. I'd thought I'd hidden it so well. Indeed, I think I have, to all but Mei. I feel vulnerable and seen, and it feels new and a bit . . . frightening.

"I've wanted to tell you," I falter. "I just . . . I know my kind is forbidden . . ."

"My father would have imprisoned you, had he known," she says gravely. "I've always wondered why you've stayed. Surely, with your cunning and skill you could have returned home?"

"I could have." I gaze up at her steadily. "I've dreamed of home every day since I was captured. When I rose through the ranks of servants to become a guard, I knew I could slip away. But I . . ." I gently place a hand on her knee. "I had reason to stay."

"Why?" she whispers, tears gathering in her eyes. "Why

would you stay for me? I'm the least accomplished of my sisters, I'm so fearful and shy, my only worth is in my marriage to a political ally . . ."

"My lady. Shhh." I smile up at her. "I love you. I've always loved you. Is that not enough?" I brush away her tears with my thumb. "About our journey. I've replenished my energy here with the . . . occasional dalliance. But in the weeks we'll be climbing the Cloud Mountains, I may weaken. I'll have the strength to get there, but I don't want you to be alarmed."

"Is there anything I can . . . do? To help? I've heard stories of fox spirits gaining strength from . . . encounters with young men . . ."

"I'd *never* ask anything of you," I say firmly. "This is why I'm telling you now, so you aren't alarmed. I would never want you to feel I'd pressured you into giving me anything you were not glad to give."

"But would it . . . work? If I were . . . If we were to . . ."

"It would," I say, trying desperately to push aside all thoughts of her silken skin. Her lips, as tempting as a ripe plum. "It's different than with a man. With men, my energy comes from the product of his arousal. With a woman, it's her pleasure itself that . . ."—I swallow thickly—"gives me life."

Mei is breathing heavier. She licks her lip quickly, the pink of her tongue just a flicker, and then gone.

"But this is all just information for you to have. I have the strength to make it to my people, and then our own ways will sustain me. I just don't want you to be alarmed, and I want you to be absolutely free of obligation. We'll be all right."

We find the stable boy in a drunken sleep, the wine I'd gifted him staining his rough-spun clothes. I saddle and lead a sturdy mare from her stall, and then climb onto her, offering Mei a hand to pull her onto the horse behind me. She wraps her arms around me without hesitation, and I savor the feel of her, pressed firm against my back.

And in the darkness of the night, we slip away.

We ride first to the shallow stream bordering her father's land, walking the mare through the shallow water for miles. The splashing of her hooves against the water and rocks is gentle in the stillness of night. I feel Mei shiver with cold.

"Hold me closer," I tell her; and she does, squeezing tighter, burying her face in my hair that trails down my back. For miles we follow the stream, any tracks we are leaving soon washed smooth by the gracious flow of the water. When the stream joins a wide, great river, we turn west, and head toward the mountains.

As the sun rises, streaks of gold glistening over the hills, Mei breaks the silence.

"Tell me about your home?"

I stroke her hand where it rests on my belly. Her fingers absently touch my cloak.

"It's been many years since I last saw my home. But my strongest memory is the smell of the air. High above the smog of cooking fires and the stink of tanning leather and chamber pots, the air is so clean and cool—it tastes of frost and the water of mountain springs. The texture of it is different too: so thin and clear, it slips through your nose like silk, or the steam from a cup of exquisite tea."

"Mmm," she hums contentedly, nuzzling against my back with her face. "Tell me more?" The sun is rising steadily, the world warming as it brightens. The light shimmers through every drop of dew.

"The trees are fewer and thinner up there. None but the

strongest survive the harsh winds, and the ones that do grow short and wide, their limbs curled and twisting."

"You have such a beautiful voice," Mei murmurs. "I feel I've spent much too little of my life listening to you speak." She adjusts her grip around my waist. The silence stretches between us, comfortable and soft.

"Sometimes, I think I've always loved you," she says quietly. Her words fill my chest with warmth. I struggle to take in air.

"The first time I saw you," I say, turning my chin toward her, "I was standing guard on the wall, and you were walking in the garden. You saw a mouse, and you swept up the nearby cat, holding it and talking to it all the while until the mouse had run safely away. And I think that's when I knew I loved you. That I wanted to give my love to someone so kind and good and beautiful."

"I remember that day!" I feel her stretch a bit behind me, resting her arms atop my shoulders. "I'd been chastised for being distracted during poetry lessons. I've always loved poetry, but struggled to compose poems out loud, in the fashion of the royal court. I preferred to sit and write them in solitude, and my tutor had become so cross with me, despairing of my ability to ever catch the eye of a suitable husband. And when I saw that mouse, I just thought . . . maybe he is misunderstood too."

I smile. The air is cold against my teeth.

"The first time I saw you," she says sleepily, hugging me close once again; I can hear that she is beginning to drift, "you were standing guard outside my father's study." Her voice gets fainter, slipping into sleep. "And I thought, I've never seen a woman so strong, and so beautiful . . ."

Her head sags against me, and I ride on in the quiet.

When she awakens, we are miles away. The river has

covered our tracks, and we'll sleep without a fire tonight. I know these woods and hills better than any, since I've taken to my fox form and roamed far.

We stop by a stream to rest, and then carry on until evening.

She sleeps soundly, wrapped in my arms. And I feel more whole and less alone than I can ever remember. I think about belonging. Of how I once belonged in the Cloud Mountains, but then felt restless, and roamed far, and came to embrace my human form and live among them. But I've never *belonged* among humans. I've always been a bit too quick, my senses too sharp; I've slowed my speed and feigned mortal clumsiness to avoid perception.

I know that Mei has never felt she belonged with her family. Her sisters are so showy in their talent, so ambitious in their aims. Her father is preoccupied with matters of state, and her mother is busy keeping her place in royal society. Mei is soft and sweet, which might be seen as weakness by some, but I see it as a quieter kind of strength. One that isn't valued by her family, but has inherent, inexplicable value to me. When you've lived in the woods as I have, every predator is fast and bold, cunning and dangerous. Among humans as well, most are striving and grasping, climbing up or pushing away. But Mei has a gift for just . . . *being*. Existing in her own space, glowing with her own light. For a creature as ready for a life of quiet as I am, her pull is strong as a river current. Holding her feels like peace.

I fall asleep, and I dream that I am my fox, sleeping by a warm fire, Mei's gentle hands buried in my white fur.

I awaken slowly, feeling the warmth of Mei beside me, and I bury my nose deeper into the fur of my tail. My tail? I must have shifted in my sleep! I worry that Mei will be frightened, but when I see her face, I realize she must have awakened before me. She's gazing at me with wonder, reaching out a single finger to touch the tip of one of my tails.

"You're awake!" she says with a smile. "Huli, my darling, you are so beautiful!" I yawn and stand, stretching my paws before me, arching my back, enjoying her admiration.

"May I?" she asks, and I step closer to her and sit, winding my tails around me, letting her take my chin in her hand. She kisses me so, so gently on my head, and I shiver with joy.

"As delighted as I would be to stare at you all day," she laughs, "we may want to get moving before the sun is high!"

I turn, and circle—once, twice; shifting to my human form on the third turn. I pull the blanket over me as I turn away, and I'm feeling for my clothes beneath me when I feel her hand on the naked skin of my shoulder.

"Wait," she says. "Can I . . . see you like this . . . too?" I slowly drop the blanket, resisting the urge to shiver in the cool morning air. My nipples prick with the chill, and I feel all at once cold yet hot under her gaze. She reaches out to touch, but stops short, her gaze roaming down my body, the full peaks of my breasts, the softness of my belly, the dark curls above my sex.

"You are so beautiful," she whispers, and it feels different. I feel seen, and desired, by this woman who is everything beautiful and good. I tremble with the intensity of it.

She leans forward, places her palm against my cheek, and kisses me. Her lips are soft and small, and her breath is warm and full of comfort. She breathes deeply as we kiss, our mouths sliding and tasting, her tongue shyly tracing the edge of my lip. I bite her lip gently with my sharp teeth, and she gasps. I feel the swell of her body, the movement, the music of it as she moves against me, and I drink in her pleasure.

Then my stomach gurgles loudly, and she pulls away, laughing.

"I'll take XiGua to the water while you get dressed!"

"XiGua?" I ask, pulling on my shirt and trousers. "Watermelon? Who named her that?"

"I did, just now!" She smiles back at me, holding the sturdy mare's lead. "Because she's round like a melon, and just as sweet!"

I can't contain my joy as I laugh, grinning up at the brightening sky.

The further Mei travels from home, the more at ease she seems. Her breaths grow deeper and slower, her body feels more relaxed against my back, and she speaks with a freedom I've never heard from her. I feel so lucky to be witness to this open, earnest side of her. It fills me with joy that I get to see her like this.

"How many lovers have you had?" she asks. I choke on the dried fig I'm swallowing, and have to take a drink of water before I can speak.

"Quite a few," I say finally. "Men and women, although men are the easiest to find."

"You are so beautiful," she says after a minute. "I've always turned my gaze away from women, especially in bathhouses. I've always been too afraid to look with . . . with *wanting*." She slides her hand under the hem of my shirt and I gasp to feel her fingers on my skin. She presses her hand against me.

"I want you," she says simply.

By evening, the terrain has grown steeper and rockier. The mountains in the distance loom large, their peaks disappearing into the clouds. I lead us to a cave I've slept in before, carefully sniffing at the entrance to ensure no animal has taken up residence in my absence. Mei sets up camp while I shift to my fox and catch a rabbit, bringing it back and shifting again to roast it over a crackling fire. I proudly present it to Mei, but she picks at it, barely pulling the meat from the bones.

"Are you all right?" I ask.

"I'm not that hungry," she says absently.

"How can you not be hungry? We've been riding all day! You need to eat, my lady."

She shivers.

"Are you cold?"

"No, I'm not, I just . . ."

"What's wrong?"

She looks at me, and her eyes are blazing with certainty. "I just . . . want you."

My breath catches. "My lady . . . I . . ."

"No, please hear me out first. Please just listen." I nod, and she continues. "I know you don't want to pressure me. I know you worry that I'll feel I owe you something, but I need you to understand—I want you. I've wanted you for so long. Every touch, every look has set a burning in my heart, and I don't want to wait any longer. *Please*, Huli. Please make love to me. Please just . . . take me. Now. *Please.*"

She's leaning into me, and when I turn toward her, she kisses me. Her kiss feels different this time. Hungrier. Less controlled. I reach out and hold her face, my hand trailing down her throat, wrapping gently around her slender neck. She moans, high and soft, and I feel her pleasure as if it were my own.

And then I'm kissing her neck. She twitches and gasps when she feels the sharp points of my teeth, so I use them more. I nip her earlobe. I trace my canines gently down her throat. She is trembling and gasping, her eyes half closed, her head thrown back. She is the most beautiful woman I've ever seen and she wants *me.* I pull her tunic aside and kiss her freckled shoulder. I scrape my teeth along her collarbone, and she threads her fingers through my hair, pressing my face to her. Every kiss brings a thrill of pleasure. A promise of things to come.

I lay her down so, so gently on the blankets. The light from the fire flickers off her face as she holds my gaze; and her face is so trusting, I'm momentarily afraid. I don't want to do anything to hurt that trust. But I know I won't. I adore her, and I'd gladly give my life to keep her safe.

She takes off her clothes unashamedly, and I drink in the sight of her. She holds my gaze proudly, like she enjoys me looking. Then she fingers the hem of my tunic. "I want to see you."

I remove my clothes, feeling her gaze on me, and then I'm laying down on top of her, our breasts pressing against each other, her head cradled in my open hand.

I spread her legs with my knee as I kiss her, and she opens for me, rocking her hips against me. I feel the wetness of her sex against my thigh. She continues to grind into me as my mouth travels down, kissing her throat, her chest . . . I pause above her small breasts, her nipples puckered and tantalizing. Then I open my mouth and breathe on her, and she gasps, writhing beneath me. I reach my tongue out to touch the tip of her nipple gently, and then a little firmer.

Rocking her nipple back and forth, I lower my mouth and suck lightly. Her moans become more plaintive, more desperate. When I graze her with my teeth, she gasps, "Oh, Huli! Yes!"

I reach my hand down and stroke my fingertips across her hips. I trail them along the delicate fuzz on her belly, through the curls of her mound, and then lower, stroking her wet slit. She grows more still as I gently ease her folds apart, stroking around her entrance, pulling her wetness up toward her bud, swirling my finger around it. Her face is full of wonder.

"Is this ok?"

"I . . . yes." Her hands gently hold my face. "You feel so beautiful," she whispers. "You *are* so beautiful. I've never felt like this, I . . ." She gasps as I slide a finger inside her. "*Huli*," she cries, "Promise me you'll never leave me. Promise me you'll stay with me."

"I promise," I breathe, and slide another finger inside her. She's so slick and warm around my fingers; every breath and sound she makes is pure pleasure to me. I slowly turn my hand, watching her face, enjoying the feel of her sex around my fingers. I curl my fingers, feeling the ridges inside her, and watch as her face changes in surprise, and awe.

"What is that?" She is trembling.

"It's a beautiful spot inside you, my lady."

"Please just . . ." She quivers around my fingers. "Don't stop . . ."

I press the pad of my middle finger firmly into her ridge, stroking up and then down. Drawing deep circles. I feel her wetness grow, flowing around my fingers, sliding down into my palm. She begins to move her hips and I angle my hand so she can grind against me. Her folds are plush, and they spread around my hand. The smell of her is overwhelming my senses, every nerve ending of my fingers is alight with the pleasure of feeling her, and she grinds harder, grows more desperate.

"Huli, I . . ."

"Yes, my lady?"

"Don't stop, I just . . . I . . . Aaaah!" She claws desperately at my back and I lean over her, kissing her temple, whispering to her as she clenches around my fingers, her wetness soaking my hand.

When her trembling slows, she sighs tremulously, and relaxes in my arms. I slide out of her and hold her, kissing her face, telling her how beautiful she is, how much I treasure her. Her hair clings to the sweat on her face, and I brush it away.

"Huli . . ."

"Yes, my lady?"

"I didn't know I could feel like this." Her hips rock beneath me.

"Can I pleasure you more, my dearest?"

"Please, yes, I . . ." She grips my face fiercely. "Teach me more," she begs.

"With pleasure, my lady." I begin to kiss my way down her body. "The more you relax," I say as I kiss along her chest, stopping to tease her nipples, "the slower and deeper your pleasure." I breathe deeply of her scent under her arms, her hair there tickling my nose.

"And the deeper your pleasure," I whisper against her belly, dragging my nose through the curls of her mound, "all the greater is my own."

She spreads her legs for me, and her sex blooms in front of me. Her bud is hidden shyly in its hood; her folds are gleaming like flower petals in the rain. I inhale deeply, breathe her scent and pleasure into me.

"May I kiss you here, my lady?" I ask.

"Mmmmm." She writhes, arching her back, panting in

anticipation. I blow gently on her sex, thrilled as she moans and trembles.

"May I?" I ask again.

"You may!" she murmurs. "Please, Huli!"

I narrow my tongue, and delicately touch her hood, sliding around it, teasing out her clit. I move slowly, deliberately, and I feel her begin to relax. Her movements slow; her breaths deepen. Shyly, her bud begins to emerge from its hood. I circle it with my tongue, gently, and then deeper, finally pressing into her and sucking. I reach up and touch her face, feel her open mouth breathe against my palm, drag my fingers down her neck.

I push my face against her, deeper, and enjoy myself more. I draw my tongue down to her entrance, and circle it, tasting her delicious juices, her flesh so soft and warm and beautiful.

"Huli?!" she whispers in wonder. "I didn't"—she pants—"know anything could feel . . . this good . . ."

"Mmmmmmmmmm," I hum against her sex, and I feel her twitch in response to the vibrations.

I lift my face to look up at her. Her head is thrown back; her mouth is open. Nothing in this world, *nothing*, is as beautiful as the bliss I see there.

"Look at me, my lady."

She lifts her head and looks down at me. Then she moans as she sees my face—my grin, her juices glistening on my chin.

"Place your hands on my head, my lady," I command gently. "Grind against my face. Take your pleasure from me."

She reaches for me, shyly, and I lower my mouth to her again, drinking deeply of her. I broaden my tongue and press it against her, rocking it up and down, side to side. I lift my face slightly and fill my lungs like I am diving underwater, then press my face against her again. This time, I feel her fingers more firmly against my scalp, and she rocks her hips gently, beginning to grind on my face. Pleasure fills me as she takes her own, ecstasy building in me as steadily as water flowing down the mountains in a spring thaw.

Extending my tongue, I press it into her as deeply as I can, her taste tangy, every fold of hers lush and delicious.

"Huli!" She gasps. "I need you . . . I . . ." Her hands grow strong against my scalp, and she pulls my hair roughly, desperately. I am awash in her, her thighs clenched around me, her sex around my face, my nose buried in her curls. I can't breathe, don't want to breathe, want to drown completely in *her*.

"Huli, I . . . aaaaah!" Her hips buck hard against me, and I rock my face from side to side, savoring her with every fiber of my being. She thrusts desperately against me once—twice—and her pleasure fills me to overflowing. As she falls back, her body damp with exertion, I move to catch her head with my hand, lowering it gently to the ground. I pull her to me, wind myself around her, and stroke her head as she drifts to sleep.

THREE

On the Edge

by Natalie Naudus and Mary Helen Gallucci

It begins as a joke. Lianne is reading her cliterature on the couch next to me while I watch reels on Instagram, and I glance down at her Kindle. Bored, I start reading over her shoulder, and poking fun.

"His sweaty shoulders? How is that sexy?"

"Babe, do not start, just let me enjoy this."

"Am I just too much of a lesbian, or is that really attractive to you?"

"It's not *unattractive . . .*"

"How? He's gotta smell ungodly."

"Well, imagine it's a woman instead."

I pause. Consider. Think about Lianne's shoulders after she's worked out, the deep divot at her spine, the rippling muscles in her arms, her upper back . . . "Oh ok. Yeah, that does work."

"My sweet baby, you are *so* gay."

"And *you* my love, are very bisexual."

We kiss, and go back to our devices. Soon enough, though,

my attention wanders back to her Kindle. "Devon? Of course his name is Devon," I snark.

"Do you need some attention or something?"

"Do I see the word 'hard' twice in one sentence? 'She took the long *hard* thick hot glorious length of him in one *hard*, swift plunge . . .' Who even wrote this?"

Lianne just sighs, throwing her legs over my lap and angling her Kindle away. I can't help but lean to keep reading.

"And what . . . oh my god what is he saying, he's . . . commanding her to come??" I start laughing so hard that Cody, our elderly beagle, startles awake from his nap.

"It's not *that* ridiculous," Lianne protests.

"Oh come on, who can actually come on demand?"

"I could," Lianne says, tossing her hair over her shoulder.

"No way," I scoff. But she doesn't back down. When she arches an eyebrow, I shift gears fast. "Wait. Could you?"

"Babe, you know I'm like . . . very orgasmic."

"No, I know but like . . . on demand?"

"If you went nice and slow, and eased off when you knew I was getting close . . . yes."

We lock eyes, a silly goofy grin spreading over both our faces. And then we are both on our feet, running to the bedroom, shirts and bras and pants scattering until we are naked in bed, Lianne wrapped around me like a koala hugging a tree.

She shimmies down to nibble at my nipple, and as she moves I feel the heat and wetness from her core against my knee. "Oh my god, babe, how did *that book* get you ready?!"

"Maybe it did, or maybe I'm just happy to see you."

"Okay, well, we have to fix that then. No getting too happy too fast, for you. Stay there."

Lianne purrs, "Oooh, bossy, I like it already . . ." as I extricate myself from her limbs and slide off the bed to dig in my top drawer. I find it—it's a long black strip of silk—and return to wrap it gently but securely around her eyes.

"No more happy to see me," I instruct.

Lianne wiggles her shoulders in excitement, and I'm tempted to shower my adorable girl in kisses—but instead I soberly remind myself to focus on the task at hand. Which is: tormenting the gorgeous naked woman on the bed before me, stretching—arching her back, arms languidly above her head, the black silk stark against her bleached-blonde hair.

Her pale nipples are broad and soft in our warm room and I decide to start there. I bend over her, gently blowing a cool stream of air on one. It takes her a moment to notice, but when she does, she gasps and squirms. "Oh my god!"

I pool saliva on my tongue before giving her a tiny lick—feather-light—so that a bead of wetness slowly drips down her nipple. I blow again, narrow and cool. Lianne moans and arches as before my eyes, the sensitive flesh contracts and gathers to a firm peak. "I heard we liked things *hard*," I murmur, and she huffs a laugh—too far under my little spell to give me the whack I would otherwise expect for such a line.

I might normally proceed to her other nipple, but tonight I let the asymmetry linger and move, careful not to touch her, above her head to the crook of her arm, just inside her elbow. I nip at the paper-thin skin there, and Lianne shrieks in surprise. "What the fuck, babe, what was that?!" she laughs.

"Love bite." She can't see me waggle my eyebrows, and that's probably just as well. Focus.

I lick, long and broad, up her armpit. Now she thrashes, her arms colliding with mine haphazardly as I hover over her. "BRITT," she squeals, "what is happening?!"

"You tell me," I purr in her ear, suppressing a chuckle. "Is it working?"

Lianne shudders. "Somehow, yes. But *please* actually touch me?"

I consider this, and climb off her. She senses my absence and moans, "Oh my god babe I said *please*, where are you going??"

"I heard you, sweetheart; I love it," I tell her from the foot of the bed. I have an idea, and I'm not sure if it's going to be a hit or a *total* ridiculous miss. First, though, I want to take stock of where she's at already: I ease her knees apart, resting myself between them. With the pads of my fingers I spread her closely-shaven lips almost clinically, and appreciate the sheen of wetness glistening on her beautiful inner folds. Then I press the heel of my hand to her mound, tugging up the hood of her clit . . . and I blow a little, for good measure.

"Briiiiitt," she groans, "*actually touch me.*"

"Okay, yes," I whisper breathily into her pussy. I'd been waiting for her to ask again. I see her clench and release expectantly.

Then I take her foot, massage the arch for a moment, and pull it to me.

We have never tried anything like this before; frankly, it has never appealed—though I've always admired her adorable toes, and they smell faintly of her fresh apple body wash—but at the moment, curiosity and the sheer wide-open opportunity of the experimental moment call to me. I slide my tongue over her big toe, then take it into my mouth.

"BABE," she gasps, with an astonished laugh that I *think* registers a thrill of delight— "*that—tickles?!* Oh my—god?!" I'm slipping my tongue into the webbing between her toes now, fluttering like I'm working between her legs, and I glance up to see her propped up on her elbows—blindfold still in place—mouth dropped open as she laugh-gasps raggedly. Her face is flushed *bright* pink, and I am having the time of my life playing this game. Her foot keeps jerking but I'm holding it tight. Now I'm nibbling on her middle toe, and the truth is, I've always said I wanted every inch of this woman, and I can't believe I've let these amazing inches elude me all this time. Every time I suck, I can almost *see* the waves of sensation running up her leg as she trembles, then squeezes her knees together.

I notice her hand drop to her stomach, then lower. Breaking my suction, I order, "Whoa, no way, baby, you cannot touch yourself yet."

Lianne groans. "You're *killing* me though!"

"That is kind of the whole point." I can't contain my proud smirk, and I'm sure she can hear it. "You know what, though? Why don't you spread yourself for me while I'm down here. I want to see how I'm doing."

Lianne's hips jerk a little, like I've hit a nerve. I know she loves to be exposed to me, and soaks up my admiration, but it's not something I usually approach quite this directly. "Are you serious?" she asks.

"Completely."

Her long fingers reach down and I notice them trembling as she opens herself. She's obviously itching to delve in and touch herself, and I thrill a little that she's following my directions with such effort. But even more thrilling: the lips she's showing me are now edging into a deeper red, thickening, and I moan at the meal before me. She's not the only one I'm teasing.

I return to her toes, loving the way her hips buck when I nip; the way her pussy clenches when I suck. Her little pinky toe is so sensitive, so delicate and delectable between my teeth, I'm tempted to *bite*—but I release her to find another snack.

Her thighs.

I scoot up the bed a little, moving her knee out wider to

give me access to the plush, velvety expanse of her inner thigh. Lianne's hips yearn towards me, and she releases the fingers spreading her to fist the bedsheets instead; I'm buried too deep in the pillow of her leg to care. I reach my hand up to flick and tweak her nipple, and she presses her breast into my hand, moaning, arching off the bed.

"Baby," I murmur, muffled. "You smell . . . incredible."

I'm dizzy with her scent—tangy, sweet, and heady—and as I move toward her other thigh, I pause at her center to inhale deeply. She shudders, and I notice a drip slipping slowly from the opening of her pussy. The tip of my nose nudges her clit and she bursts, "Britt, god, PLEASE just fucking *do it?!*"

I grin up at her. Sweat glistens on her flushed cheeks and forehead, and her lower lip is caught between her teeth, pulling through them agonizingly slowly. She doesn't know, from behind her blindfold, that I'm watching her face; and the unselfconscious need written there is *so* beautiful, I have to . . . I sneak my fingers along her folds, finding the wetness of her center, then sliding up to make a wide circle around her clit. Her lip is abruptly released as her jaw drops open and her head falls back, exposing the length of her neck. "*Thank you*," she gasps. "*MORE—PLEASE—*"

"God, baby," I murmur, enjoying a few more glimpses, a few more slick circles around her opening, her clit, her swollen lips . . . "I'm so sorry but it's too soon."

"Oh FUCK, Britt," she cries, flopping back down on the bed at the loss of my hand. I kiss that gorgeously exposed neck, then her lips. She kisses me back desperately—maybe a touch irritably.

"I love you, baby," I say against her lips.

"I love you too," she rasps a little grudgingly. "Now can you please, *please* take care of me and tell me to come?"

"Why?" I feign innocence.

"Babyyyyyy," she groans.

"How about . . . turn over."

Lianne flies to comply, absolutely ready. She buries her face in our pillow, pulling her bent knees under her so her ass is raised for me, begging. And god, she is *beautiful.* The expanse of her skin, her soft curves, her slender ankles, the line of her back, the planes of her shoulder blades, the chaotic mess of her hair . . .

I comb it with my fingers for a moment, tenderly brushing the sweat-stuck locks behind her ears and off her back . . . then I close my hand around her neck, holding her down. A moan rises from somewhere deep in her belly as I feel her strain for a moment, testing my grip. "**YES**," she bellows into the pillow. Then she turns her head to the side to say, "Baby, *please* just take me, I am all yours. *Please.*"

"I—*love*—you begging," I tell her, and glide my other hand down her back, over the smooth curve of her ass, and into the heat of her center.

She groans wordlessly before panting, "Thank you . . ."

I run my thumb up her slit, then down, gathering and spreading her wetness, dipping a knuckle inside. She's *so* warm, I'm desperate for the feel of her on my fingers . . . and . . . But that will have to wait. I have a plan now.

I slip my slender little pinky finger inside her, hooking and probing for a second; then pull it out. "Brittan*yyyyyyyyyy*," she groans into the pillow. "MOOOORE."

"It's not up to you, baby," I remind her, stroking her neck with my thumb as I hold it.

She groans again, and I replace my pinky with my middle finger. I find and rub her G-spot, loving the eager squeeze I get in response. She's so wet, I slip out of her and slide two fingers back in—exploring, digging deeper, stroking the velvet of her walls.

I pick up my pace, and soon we're both humming with urgency. "Please, Britt," she says, "my clit—*please*—"

"You can touch it," I say, but a moment after her fingers fly to work with mine between her legs—as she's holding her breath, straining against my hands—I remind her, "but don't come yet."

"FUCK," she howls, abruptly jerking her hips to the side and away from my ministrations. I release her neck. "But I'm *so close*," she cries. "I need—agggh." She sits up and scowls under her blindfold. "Who even *are* you, babe? Jesus Christ, you understood the assignment."

I smile, *very* pleased, and kiss her forehead, pulling her close. She finds my chin and cups it, then kisses me heatedly. I can taste her frustration as her tongue strokes hard into my mouth, assertive for a rebellious moment. Then she gropes my chest, squeezing my breast; she finds my nipple and *tugs*.

I nip her tongue. "Ohhhh no you don't, babe!! I am not done with you yet, you are still mine."

Lianne giggles, clearly pleased with my playful scolding. "Yes," she murmurs happily, "yes ma'am."

I kiss her once more, then lay her back on the bed. Giving her nipples a little tug—she asked for it—I move down between her legs. She opens so wide, so eagerly, I laugh affectionately and kiss her knee. Then I settle down into my happy place, and stroke my tongue, wide and flat, up her slit. And oh, holy fuck, she tastes like a *dream*. Her folds are so swollen, and her hips drive her against my face so firmly, she melds with my mouth as I press my tongue into her deeper, *deeper* . . . She's bucking and I'm riding along, then slipping up to suck on her clit, when she cries, "Babe, I'm gonna—"

I release her. "No!!"

"Are you—*fucking* kidding me?!" she wails, leaning up on her elbows, looking murderous.

I know it's hideous to say your girlfriend looks cute when she's mad—I know it. It's gross. But I just . . . really need to see this face. I untie the blindfold, and she blinks, her pupils swiftly narrowing on me between her legs.

"Oh my *god* you are *so smug!*" she accuses, slipping into indignant laughter.

"Are you having a good time?" I ask.

"NO," she yells immediately. Then she rolls her eyes. "Yes, *obviously.* I had no fucking idea what I was getting into, though, Christ on a cracker."

"Lay back again," I say. "I didn't mean to stop that abruptly, just—hold it off, okay? I'll be gentler."

"Okaaay . . ." she mutters skeptically.

I nuzzle against her clit, and touch a light kiss to it. Lianne shudders. "Don't you dare," I warn her, and she moans.

"I'm trying. You're making it hard on purpose."

"I thought we wanted it *hard.*" I smile up at her wickedly. She groans. Then I return to her clit. I roll the tip of my tongue over it—flicking, fluttering, sucking—until I feel her tension building, her hips rising, and I soothe it, broad and gentle. I lap at the tiny bud, tuck my tongue under her hood, tease it side to side. She moans, and I soothe it again. My eyes are closed, and I've lost any sense of time, just enjoying this most intimate connection: the way she trembles at my every flutter, the sounds emanating from her throat. My mouth waters with the erogenous pleasure of her tender flesh inside it, against my lips. I could spend the rest of my life here, worshiping her, and be perfectly, blissfully content.

But. I must remember that that is not the plan tonight.

The next time she starts to build, I don't immediately soothe. Instead, I lick my fingers, and press one—then two—

inside her. She arches off the bed, crying out at the unexpected gratification. "Oh my god baby, *thank you*—"

Her pussy has relaxed so deeply under my ministrations, she easily takes my third finger too, and I stroke into her, rubbing her swollen clit with my thumb until she groans, "Now? *Please?*"

"Not yet," I tell her. I add my fourth finger, feeling her stretch around the top of my palm as I press deeper, the wetness from her and from my mouth making my base knuckles slip in like they were designed for this.

"*Britt*—" There's a desperation rising in Lianne's voice that I haven't heard yet tonight . . . or possibly ever? "I can't— hold on—much longer—baby—"

I fold my thumb into the palm of my hand, and slide the whole thing, slowly, sensitively, inside her. She moans, low and feral, as I fill her, and her whole body stills. I turn my hand ever so slightly, and she gasps; trembles.

"Please," she whispers.

"Yes," I whisper back. "Come for me, baby. Now."

And she does. It's instantaneous: she clenches so tight around my hand, pulsing and gasping, it's all I can do to move with her as she writhes. I can't tell when one orgasm ends and another begins; we're riding wave after wave until she's panting, almost crying, limp and spent.

Afterwards, we're lying in bed, sated, smelling like sex.

"So, you *can* come on demand," I say, impressed. "Who'da thunk. *So* glad I know this now, wow."

"My book has some other good ideas, if you wanna check it out . . ."

"Ooh, like what?"

Lianne hesitates. "Y'know what, let's sleep first. You just fully murdered me, and somehow I think you'll find a way to rally and do it again if I tell you more."

I yawn. "Fair enough. Guess it's a pretty good book."

FOUR

Mother Superior

by Mary Helen Gallucci

*D*ONGGGG

As the bell clangs the last of its twelve times and we reflexively rise as one, I spot a movement out of the corner of my eye. It's Sister Grace, our novice, hustling to her place and pulling the little prayer book from the pocket deep within her habit. Her thumb shuffles deftly through its pages until it falls open to the service of Nones. The book's pages are worn thin and soft, but not by her—that prayer book had belonged to Sister Angelica for seventy-seven years before she died. Right there in the cot given to Grace when she appeared at our convent a few days later.

She hasn't memorized the litany yet, then. As my mouth forms the familiar words, I find myself watching her eyes scanning the page. They're veiled by long lashes, sharp and bright, still, with novelty. But there's something unsettling in them; something I haven't identified in another woman for a long while. Not since I was transplanted from the abbey of my youth to serve as abbess of this community of aging gentlewomen. It's not sadness—that is a soft thing I would recognize. Nor boredom; I'd know that too.

As I ponder, her eyes dart up to meet mine, and flare. In that moment I see it: *anger.*

A shudder runs through me, involuntarily. The fire in her eyes *burns* into mine. It's so *alive,* I feel like it's jumped the distance across the small sanctuary and skittered across my skin so that every hair stands on end.

I rub my arms against the goosebumps there, smoothing my garments over my chest where I'm shocked to feel the hard nubs of my nipples, protruding almost painfully under the fabric. Abruptly, I register several sisters eying me with concern, I've lost the thread of the prayer, my mouth ajar but forming no words.

Forcing my head clear, I resume the song of supplication, and make two mental notes. First, I must scold Sister Grace for her tardiness. Second, I *must* explore that spark deep within her—she has come to me for a reason, I feel suddenly certain, and I burn with a frenetic interest I'd forgotten my soul could feel.

But there is a little voice, ringing in my ears with the hymn, that insists upon adding another note. Third: I must avoid this girl at all costs.

The next time I come upon Sister Grace, we are dressed down and heading from our beautifully manicured grounds out to the stables, where we must milk the cows before each engaging in our daily duties to produce our convent's cheese. The sisters form a neat row, calm and patient, exchanging a friendly word or two while dutifully traipsing through the muck towards the stables. All of them, that is, but one. I can scarcely make her out in the pre-dawn haze that follows Lauds.

Having doubled back, I approach Sister Grace on the stone path outside the chapel—as far as she's gotten. She's crouched over a puddle in a divot within the stone, her habit sodden, gently scooping earthworms who've been stranded there from last night's rain. She deposits one on a flowerbed, and then looks up at me.

She doesn't startle, and I'm astonished to read no contrition on her face. She says nothing, yet I feel affronted by her hard look in contrast with her tender action. That little voice rings a warning in my ears, but I dismiss it easily: she is my novice, after all. I would be remiss to avoid her. It would be uncompassionate. Besides, the way she is cupping the earthworms in her slim, soft palm . . . If it's a disobedience, it is at least a . . . beautiful one. Still, I try to suffuse my voice with an appropriate sternness.

". . . Sister Grace," I begin, but she interrupts.

"Gray."

"Excuse me?"

"I want to be called Gray."

I find myself at a loss for words. "Gray" is not a canonical name, or virtue . . . but instead of protesting, I hear myself concede, "Sister . . . Gray."

"Not 'Sister.'"

"Excuse me?" I repeat, dumbly.

Her eyes flare again, and as in the chapel, I'm abruptly chilled. I shudder. Her eyes follow my hands as I smooth them over myself.

"I am not your *sister.* I'm just Gray."

". . . Gray," I repeat.

"Thank you," she says firmly. Then she visibly relaxes a bit. "Thank you," she whispers again.

"You're . . . you're caring for God's creatures very kindly," I observe, hoping I might continue to soften the young woman with understanding. "Your love for Him is evident."

"No," she says, nestling a worm between trimmed blades of grass. "I don't care for your 'God.' I just like earthworms."

"My—" Now I am truly gaping. I'm not sure if I'm insulted or just stunned at her candor. "Then why are you here?"

"I came to escape my family. My father insisted I marry a man."

"Was he so bad?" I ask.

Derision distorts her face, and I'm startled to notice that I find her absolutely beautiful, nevertheless. "He was a *man.*"

The way she's looking at me, it's like she can see straight through my eyes and read the thoughts etched on the inside of my skull. It's chilling. She's . . . captivating. I've never met anyone like her.

"Perhaps you . . . understand?" she ventures softly, peering into me.

I force my eyes closed. "Certainly . . . certainly not." Gathering myself, I harden my tone. "Now, see that you join your —the—sisters in the stables at once—Gray. You have duties there, to—well, if not God, then I suppose to . . ."

"You," she supplies. Then she stands. "Thank you, Mother Veronica, for using my name. For seeing me."

Her words melt something low in my belly, and I pray my face hasn't flushed visibly—and that my scapular hides the way my nipples are pricking in the morning's chill. I've been standing idle for too long; I turn on a heel and hasten off ahead of her.

I've tried all day to push away thoughts of that woman, but her face—her lashes, the tilt of her chin, the sharp gray of her eyes—is burnt indelibly into my mind. Every time I close my eyes—every time I blink, she's there. Staring into me with that rebellious fire that melts me to my core.

By the time I reach my cell after Compline, my undergarments are soaked. *I'm sorry*, I send up a hasty prayer, *but I must.* I shut the door behind me and, leaning against it, pull my arm in through the layers of my habit until my cool fingers find the warm flesh of my belly. I slide them down, heaving a sigh of relief as they find my swollen, drenched folds.

Sensation floods through me as my fingertips revel in the warmth, the slickness, and I circle my clit, stifling a moan. I've slumped, opening to myself, until I'm on my knees on the tile floor, braced on one hand while my other delves into me.

My fingers slip inside me and I'm pressing down onto them, the back of my hand inside my habit grinding against the floor as I push, wanting deeper. I feel *so* good, hot and wet and then, god help me, I'm envisioning her face—

It's the way she said "You," penetrating me with her eyes. It's the way she inseminated me with her spark . . . the way she spoke to me without reverence and thanked me for— something unholy, for—being *me*. Like she *knew* what she was touching within me, like she could *see* my body reacting to her, like I was naked under all the heavy fabric.

The ache in my nipples becomes too much; rolling over, I bring my other hand inside to find my breast. I pinch myself and tug, remembering how she had watched me smooth myself over—her eyes had been, for a moment, on my chest, and what if she *wanted*—

My fingers are becoming frantic inside me, my palm against my clit, and it bursts through me like a revelation that *I want—I want—her—*

I bite my lip against a scream as my climax overwhelms me, and in my mind's eye, I think I see her lips quirk a smile.

At Lauds the next morning, she isn't there.

My mind is racing as the opening phrases of morning prayers unfurl—what did I say to her? Did I frighten her? She hadn't seemed like the kind of person to be distressed by a little chastisement, and besides, I had been specifically trying for kindness before . . . before I lost control of myself. If anyone was cowed, I'm fairly certain, it was me. Is she testing me? Asserting her will to see if I'd—what, punish her for disobedience?

At that moment, she rushes in. Spotting me, she aims herself in my direction, and sidles in beside me. "I'm sorry, Mother," she whispers.

I give a sharp jut of my chin that I hope communicates "not now." I gesture to the pocket where she keeps her prayer book and hiss, "Pray."

She glances down at herself in confusion for a moment, before slipping out the book and opening it. Her voice is clean and clear as it joins the sisters', and I find myself singing softer to listen. She is standing so close, I can smell the faint scent of the lye soap that she's used on her skin. I wonder what her hair is like, under her veil. Her hip brushes mine absently and

I flush, but am careful to keep my eyes on the crucifix at the front of the chapel.

I'm sorry, I think at it, remembering my actions last night. But I can sense her body heat beside me, in a way I've never once noticed from any of the other sisters here in the chapel day and night, and the thought feels suddenly slippery. *I'm sorry*, I think again—*I am sorry; Jesus Christ, son of God, have mercy on me, a sinner.* I repeat that "prayer of the heart" insistently in my head, giving steady battle to my persistent thoughts of the woman next to me—*right* there, a breath away—until the service ends.

Then she turns to me. "Mother Veronica," she begins, "I'm sorry I was late."

I'm fully prepared to forgive her tardiness (I'd forgotten about it), the sooner to dismiss her to her duties and, more importantly, to avoid being on the receiving end of electricity in front of the crucifix—again. My grasp on my feelings of contrition toward it feels tenuous at best, as it is. "Just don't make it a habit," I tell her dismissively, and turn away.

She takes my elbow. "Don't you need to punish me?" From her voice, I understand her question to mean that she feels guilty, and wishes to curb her passions into obedience. But when I see that damned glint in her eye, my confidence wavers.

"N-no, Sister," I say and she flinches. "—Gray," I correct myself.

"What if—what if I hadn't come at all?"

"I suppose it would've been my duty to seek you out."

"Not—punish me?"

I can't keep the fluster out of my tone. "The *Lord* punishes, and there is penance due to him if you wish to . . . honor *that* debt, but it wasn't my understanding that your heart was . . . aligned to such matters."

"Ah," she says, a smile tugging at her lips. Then, softly: "Wish it was you."

And with that, she vanishes.

Gray attends Prime, Terce, Sext, Nones, and Vespers as she should—arriving early, in fact, and standing in her proper position among her peers. But just when I'm thinking that I'd imagined that conversation in the sanctuary . . . the tower bell rings in Compline, and she's nowhere to be seen.

"O God, come to my assistance," I intone, initiating the service.

"O Lord, make haste to help me," the Sisters respond on their pitch.

What if I hadn't come at all? Gray had asked. What had I said? I'd promised I would find her. But my head is swimming. That warning voice in my ear is *certain* this is a terrible idea, and it's buzzing like bees weaving through the air with the chant, the incense, the candle smoke. Another voice says, but it is my duty to seek her out. And another, from somewhere deep down, says—I *want* to seek her out.

The other sisters have noticed her absence as well, and nod in understanding when I bow my head to them, then hasten out of the chapel, into the dark.

The first place I look is the dormitory. It is night, and the life of a nun is a grueling one to adapt to. It is entirely to be expected that she may have returned to change out of a soiled habit, and simply fallen asleep from exhaustion. I remind myself to exercise patience, and compassion, as I would with any other Sister new to the order.

—Any other *woman*, I correct myself. Gray does not wish to be called Sister. I'm not sure where she finds the permission to make such declarations; my authority has not otherwise been challenged since I arrived here, and I'm unaccustomed to disputes. She must, I can only surmise, request and receive the permission from . . . herself?

I've arrived at the door to her cell, and I knock. "Gray? Are you asleep?"

"No." Her voice cuts through the door, crystal clear.

I hesitate for a moment. "You . . . aren't at Compline."

She opens the door. "Neither are you."

I'm not sure which has me more dumbstruck—the boldness of her retort, or the way the candlelight behind her illuminates her dark hair, unveiled. It's in a thick rope of a braid, but the escaped wisps frame her face like a natural halo.

"Come in," she says, finally. "Please. I *must* be punished."

"Gray—" I begin, but my throat feels tight and the words die on my lips as she takes my hand, pulling me in.

"Please," she says again. Then she shuts the door behind me.

I'm momentarily distracted by the room—the drab little cell that just last week was bare and sparse and uniform—because she's peppered it with such surprising beauty, I think for a moment I've left the monastery all together. She's got flowers tucked in every nook and cranny, a bright patchwork quilt on the bed, a little silver hand mirror (absolutely not permissible on the grounds) and a rough clay statuette of a . . . of a woman's figure . . .

I feel Gray step close behind me as I gape. "Do you think she's beautiful?"

". . . Yes," I admit.

"I made her," she tells me.

"Gray," I breathe.

"You keep saying my name," she says, her eyes shining in the candlelight. I can't help staring at them—at her lips, so near—at the stray hairs across her cheek. Despite myself, I reach to brush them behind her ear, and she sighs at the contact, catching my hand in hers. She leans her cheek into my palm, then turns her lips to it.

Her kiss in my palm could be chaste, despite the way it makes me flush so warm, I glance to the candle to ensure that the fire isn't spreading. But then she moves to my wrist, and the moan that my betraying lips emit is most certainly nothing modest.

Our mouths meet fervently. Her lips are brave and earnest against mine, searching, delighting; a laugh bubbles from my chest as my hands tangle in her mess of hair. She deftly slips my veil from my head, then frees my hair from my bandeau so it falls about my shoulders. "Yessss," she whispers; then her tongue darts out to taste mine, licking and sucking on my lower lip.

"Yes?" I pant.

"I *knew* you understood me," she laughs. Then she adds, "Mother."

I shudder against her, and she holds on tighter, then urges me toward her cot. It's narrow, and low to the floor, and when my calves reach it I stumble backward to sit on it.

Gray takes a step back, and begins stripping off her robes. I'm transfixed. I can't look away, much as I know I should. I don't *want* to. And from her smile, her proximity, her confidence . . . I understand that she doesn't want me to, either. Never have I appreciated each layer of our habit with such an admiring eye: the way the scapular crests and falls over her breasts, until it is lifted off. The way the belt cinches her waist, and hangs in a V low over her abdomen, the ends draping over her thigh and between her legs—until it is untied. The way the tunic sweeps over her hips, and offers glimpses of her narrow ankles as it brushes them, until it is removed. The sheerness of her light cotton slip, in the candlelight; the way it falls across her thighs, now bare. I'm barely breathing.

Slowing only slightly, Gray removes her undergarments until she stands before me unabashedly, the light flickering and licking across her bare skin. She's loosened her hair so that it falls across her shoulders and chest, rosy nipples peeking through. Her breasts cast shadows across her middle; her navel is like a dark pool, running to the curls between her legs.

I'm still staring as she turns, and then falls to her knees, bowing in deep oblation toward the crucifix on her wall. Her face is pressed to the tile floor, her arms outstretched . . . and her pale bottom is bared to me, hovering just above her heels, glowing in the candlelight. Then I hear her voice, low and grave: "Forgive me, Mother, for I have sinned."

I swallow, then hear myself say slowly, in a voice not my own: "There—there is nothing to forgive."

"Yes," she insists. "You came to correct my sin. I owe penance. You must . . . help me. Save my soul."

"H-how?" I stammer, enthralled.

"Flagellation."

"I . . . I don't have the . . . the tools—" I'm trembling at the very idea.

"Your h-hand, then," she grates evenly, only a quaver betraying thinly veiled desperation. In the shadow between her cheeks, my eye catches on something wet, glistening.

My mouth is dry as a wafer.

"Please," she rasps. "You must."

A moment passes in absolute silence; she doesn't move, doesn't relent. She is waiting.

I have risen from the bed and knelt behind her, but my

eyes won't lift as they should to the cross. I am mesmerized—intoxicated by the vision before me.

I lift my hand—suspend it midair.

"Do it."

My palm falls on her right cheek, the sound echoing about the cell's stone walls.

She flinches; then she offers me her other cheek, straining toward my uplifted hand.

"Purge—me," she gasps between my strokes. "Cleanse—me—Mother." Her cheeks are a darkening red in the low light, hot under my hand. I strike again. And again. Harder. My hand has become slick with sweat. She shudders, then moans: "Mine—is—eternal—fire—"

I pause as long, slender fingers slither out from the shadows beneath her, knit themselves among her folds, and begin working there between her legs, frantic. I'm bowed to them, staring in wonder—holy adoration—as she rubs and writhes, displayed before me.

Finally, she keens, her hand stilling, her hips jerking—and then again. She releases a sigh and withdraws her sodden fingers. Then she lies there, spread and panting.

After a long moment, I find my voice. "Gray," I begin, hesitant.

She turns to me. "Yes," she says huskily, "thank you."

"You're . . . I—" I retreat, lifting myself off the floor and finding a seat again on her cot.

"Let me thank you for using my name," she urges.

"You—already have," I rasp, as she centers herself between my knees, then pushes them apart. "It's just a name."

"It isn't," she says firmly. "This is . . . who I want to be. Who I am." I swallow as she lifts the hem of my robe. "Is this okay? Mother?"

"Y-yes," I choke.

She bows her head, dipping under the heavy layers of my habit, and between my swollen folds, to press her mouth to my throbbing center.

I hear a cry before I register that it's me. This part of me that's been hidden so long I had thought it was forgotten . . . it's roaring to life with Gray's tongue fanning the flames. She's moaning her enthusiasm as she delves into me, lapping eagerly as I feel myself dripping against her lips, her nose, her chin . . .

I fall back on my elbows, opening to her, and my eye catches a flicker of light on the crucifix over the door. *I'm . . . I'm just not sorry*, I think, only to realize I've groaned it aloud, too overcome to pretend any guilt at this moment. *I'd do this forever.*

Gray breaks her suction to grin up at me, her eyes and bosom gleaming, and suddenly I need her to see me. All of me. She sees my fingers begin to fumble with my robes and jumps in to help, ripping the heavy fabric between the two of us until it crumples off the cot, onto the floor in tatters. I feel her eyes on me, hungry, thirsty, and I feel blessed more than any angel or saint I've ever uttered a prayer to that I'm here, partaking in this delicious communion.

Then Gray crawls over me on the cot and I reach for her breast, guiding it into my mouth and sucking hard. Her nipple slides over my tongue—I realize my mouth has been watering, and this sensitive flesh is the best thing that I've ever tasted. Gray's back arches sensually, and I'm skimming my hands over her back, her thighs, her other breast . . . I slip one hand around her long neck, briefly, and she gasps sharply before my fingers find her jaw, then her open mouth. She sucks them in and it's my turn to gasp, stunned by the warmth and wetness, the softness of her tongue, the squeeze that reminds me of— myself, just last night.

I pull my fingers from her mouth and reach them down, between her parted legs. The folds I find there are open and delicate, completely unlike mine have ever felt beneath my habit. She moans and leans into my slick fingers, and I circle them around her clit as I've done alone—marvelling at the arch of her neck, the gyration of her hips, the transformation of her beautiful face now overtaken by bliss.

I turn us, so that she's on her back on the narrow cot, and I'm now hovering over her. I feel her eyes prick along my skin as I rise and lift her leg over my shoulder, centering on her so we're heat to heat, flesh to flesh. I press myself to her center, and she reaches down to spread herself—then me—and by god I'm grinding against her like I was made for this very moment, holding her leg in one hand and my own hair atop my head in the other.

Writhing beneath me, Gray moans, "Mother . . . goddess . . ."

I know—I know—I'm supposed to hear those words as sacrilege, but all I feel is *right*, and *good*, and maybe even *holy*. Me—holier than I've ever felt in my soul.

Remembering her gasp from earlier, I release my hair and reach for her, trailing my fingers across her breast, her collarbone, until they rest gently at her throat.

"Yes please," she pants, "take me—"

I rise on my knees, pushing the leg I'd held off the edge of the cot, and sliding my fingers into her warmth, where my own had just been. I press and feel, relishing her texture, curling and flexing my fingers while she shudders under me. She's so wet and arching into me so urgently, I add a third finger; and the feel of her holding me, squeezing me, *wanting* me, is nothing if not divine. She grabs a fistful of her quilt, cramming it against her mouth to suppress her scream as I thrust into her.

I move my hand from her throat to her mouth, clasping it across her gorgeous lips, my fingers spanning her cheekbones to her jaw . . . her breath is wet on my palm as she cries out against it and then shudders, melting over my fingers, tensing and arching for a long moment, straining against both my hands. I release her mouth and she gasps; then every muscle in her body relaxes, and her eyes gleam up at me.

"Mother. Superior," she pants.

I huff a laugh. "If you're not a Sister, I don't know . . . that it makes sense for you to call me that."

"Oh," she says with a grin, "It does."

FIVE

Cozy Morning

by Mary Helen Gallucci

I'm lying in her arms. I'm not sure if I've been awake for minutes or hours. The sun is peeking through the curtains, turning my eyelids rosy when they drift closed. It's so warm here, tangled up like this under the covers, not quite sure where she ends and I begin. I feel her breathing, slow and humid, against the back of my neck, and I'm cocooned, her leg between mine. Her palm covers my breast.

Everything is perfect—or, has been, as I've been blinking in and out of sleepy awareness. But now I find that I'm waiting, very patiently I think, for something. For her fingertips to move, to wake up enough to explore me. Once I notice I'm hoping for it, I have to suppress the urge to wiggle restlessly. Her palm just presses sleepily against me as we shift against the bedsheets, squeezing a little as if to say *good morning, I love you*, not . . . *I'm ready to fuck.*

But it's ok, I'm being patient. I am. I turn in her arms, finding her beautiful face slack with sleep, so peaceful, and I press a kiss to her forehead. *Good morning,* my fingers say to her cheek, brushing across it. A smile quirks at the corners of her lips. She hums contentedly.

I take this as encouragement. My hand slides into, then under the waistband of the boxers she's been sleeping in. I squeeze her ass—oh my god it is so warm and delicious in my hand—*good* morning *baby*. My palm glides up and down, inside her boxers. Across. Up her back. I finger the dimples above her waistline, then slip under the elastic again. *Good morning baby, I love you. Maybe I want you, y'know, if you're awake and up for it. Maybe, whatever it's chill I'm chill. It's just good morning.*

Her hand finds its place on my breast and squeezes gently again. She nuzzles into my neck, kisses me. I'm so wet already and she might just be snuggly, half asleep? We might be here like this for hours yet, but I swear I am fucking patient.

Then her hand drifts to my other breast, and I can't help but press myself into her palm. She's smiling dreamily again, her eyes still closed. But she knows my body by heart, and finally her palm lifts and her fingers begin to graze my skin, swirling little circles, following the line under my breast, smoothing across my sternum. Gentle scratches, wide circles around the circumference. Is she teasing? It might be coming, I think. Maybe. I kiss her lips. *Good morning beautiful. I love you.* I kiss her again, and she hums a tiny moan. Yesss. Her lips are so soft, so relaxed. I love her.

Her fingertips are drifting, drifting. I kiss her jaw. *I love you.* I slide my hand down, out the bottom of her boxers to feel her thigh, so warm and soft. Pulling back up I maybe brush her inner thigh a little closer, a little slower. It is so warm. *Good morning beautiful, I want you. Y'know, if you. Are ready. Sometime.*

Her thumb brushes over my nipple but it's an accident, I think. It's so gentle, I *think* it happened, I *hope*, but . . . my skin is singing, sensitive—and then there it is again, just a brush. And again—she's pinching my nipple now, it's happening, she's turning me on on purpose, she knows it. She's smirking and her eyes are open now. *Good* morning *baby.*

Her fingers graze and pinch and tug until my own eyes flutter shut and I'm biting my lip to keep back my moan because *I'm sorry baby you* just *woke up and I'm at like an 11 over here.* My hips are twitching because heat has pooled inside my underwear, and I can feel the liquid squeezing down as her fingers work. I'm so easy for her. *I just* want *you, I'm sorry, I'm fucking ready.*

She knows. She's grinning at me now, the laziness turned to playfulness, and she rolls on top of me, her luscious thick hair curtained around our faces. She kisses me, hard, and my hips rock against hers before she shifts down to cover my breast with her mouth.

Now I can't help it: I moan, *oh my god yes,* and she looks up at me with wide sparkling eyes as she tongues my nipple. She's teasing it back and forth, up and down with the tip of her tongue, then sucking it in, pressing it to the roof of her mouth, rolling it between her lips.

I'm thrashing. Her hand has found my other nipple and she's teasing it in tandem, pulling and twisting and flicking and holy god I *love* wanting her so much, it's exquisite torture and I'm drenched, my legs spread for her *anytime,* my clit throbbing.

"Baby please," I manage. "I'm so wet."

"I know," she's released me to say, grinning. Yes, of course she knows what she's doing. But she just rises to kiss my jaw, licking and sucking, her fingers still working on my nipple. A little harder and I can barely stand it; her mouth is fire on my throat.

I shove my hands back into her boxers, grabbing her ass cheeks and squeezing, hard, because I'm desperate and fuck I want to pull her open. Then I palm her pussy and it's hot and damp and she's pressing against my hand but she's taller than I am and I can barely reach from this angle. My fingertips grope for her clit, slipping among her folds and she's groaning and *baby I fucking love you, I fucking adore you, you are perfect, PLEASE fucking touch me.*

Oh shit, I said that out loud, and she's cackling, sleepily but evilly.

Then her mouth is back on my goddamned nipple, and it's sensitive as hell and I think maybe it's my clit the way I feel her tongue, electric, all over my body, everywhere that counts.

Then two of her fingers brush against my lips, pressing, and I realize they're seeking entrance. I open for her and she's filling my mouth, her fingertips sliding down my tongue and I open my jaw, my throat, to take her deeper. Her fingers taste so fucking good, I could eat her, swallow her, and I love her inside me, want her inside me *goddamn it,* this is not everything but it's a lot.

She turns her wrist so now she's feeling the ridges of my palate, rubbing them "come hither" and I feel it in my g-spot, except I'm squeezing empty down below. I suck on her fingers, hard—she laughs a little, low and lazy, and murmurs, "Mmm, you like that?" But then she groans in earnest when I suck them in deeper so she's touching parts of me I'm not sure anyone has touched ever and *I love it, please know me, explore me, yes.*

She has her legs wrapped around one of mine now, and I feel her grinding against my thigh, hot and rough. We're sweaty, our skin sticking to skin. When I relent with my suction, she pulls out and I gasp, "Please touch me, baby, now."

But she just fucking nips at my nipple, squeezing the other *hard* now, twisting it and I might fucking explode?? My panties are so sodden, the bed is wet, and I know it is not all sweat.

I can't stand just lying here taking this, and I finally thrust my own hand between her legs and my thigh, finding her soaked too. "Yesssss," I hiss with delight, and shift my focus from my own frustration to the gratification of her being exactly where I'm at after all. I press my finger into her, both of us groaning at the warm glide, and urge it deeper with the strength of my thigh against my hand.

With her teeth still framing my nipple, I'm hyper-aware of her every movement as her hips rock, fucking my hand. And then her own hand slides off my breast and down my ribs, my belly, my mound . . .

"Fuuuuck me," she groans when her fingers dip in, finally, *finally*, and I'm not empty anymore and it's *perfect*, she's *perfect*, I need to scream but I can't catch a breath, my chest is so full, I'm so full. We move together, full of each other, and—her hot slick velvet against my fingers, my clit and g-spot singing together, her hair and her scent and the way her lips part as she pants—it's better than heaven.

When we've finished—of course we've not *really* finished —and as she sprawls beside me, I find I'm desperately overdue to taste her breasts. I take her in my mouth and she laughs at my eagerness and then moans at the sensation, and when her back arches I know I'm working her up again and it's *thrilling*.

"Baby," I mumble against her, "you awake enough to sit on my face?"

She looks down at me, her eyes alight. "*Mmmmmmm*hm," she affirms enthusiastically, then kisses me before rising to her knees and crawling up me.

And fuck if the view isn't *divine*, her knees wide and breasts so round and proud from this angle. The slanting morning sun glistens off her folds as I spread them with my fingers, drinking her first with my eyes. Their pink is blushing red, still swollen and relaxed from our lovemaking moments before. Her scent is exquisite. I drink that in too, inhaling deeply before I pull her hips down and bury myself in her. Then all I know is my tongue, suction and release, and the matchless flavor of her, her movement against me and her muffled gorgeous sounds. When she starts to lose control, I can't breathe and I don't want to; I hold her tighter, with my arms around her thighs and my splayed fingers and my lips on her clit, as she bucks—and I'm not sure if she's riding my mouth or if I'm the one being carried along, her ecstasy blurring with my own.

"Ohhh my god," she huffs after, collapsing on my chest, languid. "Good *morning* baby."

I hum a little, so happily, and thread my fingers through her hair. "Good morning, sweetheart. I thought you'd never wake up."

"I might just go back to sleep on you," she mumbles against my chest. "What time is it?"

I check my phone. "A little after eight."

"Oh my god, you woke me up so early?!"

"I did *not* wake you up! I was *so* patient!" I insist, not a little indignant.

"Oh yeah," she drawls. "Sooo patient, that's you."

"Hmph," I huff, and can't help but laugh a little with her. "Yes, I am."

Her weight on my chest is so calming, her hair so silky against my fingers, that I'm almost disappointed when she props her chin up to ask me, "What's for breakfast?"

"I already ate," I tell her, waggling my eyebrows.

"Har har, good one."

I offer, "I'll make you an omelet? Is this a coffee day?"

"Mmmm," she considers, resting her head again, her ear

back between my breasts. "I think just tea. Don't have much I need to get done today, can we just relax?"

"Whoa, who are you and what have you done with my girlfriend?"

"And what about . . . French toast?"

"You aren't worried about the carb coma either?? You actually *are* taking a holiday!"

"I mean"—she plants a kiss on my sternum, then snuggles deeper into me, like she might nuzzle her cheek right into my beating heart—"it is Christmas."

"Oh shit," I laugh. "I forgot! I'm like a little kid, waking you up at the crack of dawn on Christmas morning. Sorryyy . . ."

"Mmmm," she sighs dreamily. "Great presents. Worth it."

I lie under her in peaceful silence for a few minutes, petting her head slowly, my body sated and perfectly contented. Finally I whisper, "Baby, was I making French toast?" But she's drifted back to sleep.

SIX

Yes, Captain

by Natalie Naudus

"While I do admit that our cautionary window for research and observation has been completed," Dr. Onyx concludes, "I believe it my duty as chief scientist to advise further caution. The information we have collected from the probes looks favorable, but we can't rule out the possibility of anomalous conditions. I recommend another full cycle of observation and research."

"Thank you, Dr. Onyx; your recommendation is noted." I nod curtly at Dr. Onyx, and she acknowledges me with a slight dip of her head. She sits further back from the table than the rest of the officers there, her rounded belly straining against the lower bodice of her uniform. I look around the meeting table, sensing the dissent among my crew.

"Officer Dutta, do you have anything to add to the briefing?" I ask. Dutta clears her throat and sits up straighter, her annoyance palpable.

"Captain, from a security standpoint, we've been beyond cautious." Officer Dutta raps her fingers impatiently on the table. "All our probes have performed as expected, save for the one sensor malfunction, which is well within the margin for error. All planetary readings are well within acceptable levels, and even Dr. Onyx herself admits the conditions are favorable. It's time we sent down a landing party."

"Captain," Dr. Onyx addresses me. "While sending a landing seems justifiable, there were some unexpected drops in temperature that would merit an additional period of observation. I'd prefer to run some additional models . . ."

"Doctor," Officer Dutta interrupts with a sneer, "I understand your desire for a delay to the landing, but can you concede that we need to consider what's best for the entire ship, not just you and your condition—"

I raise a hand to stop Dutta's inappropriate line of questioning, but Dr. Onyx beats me to it, her demeanor calm but forceful, her hazel eyes flashing dangerously.

"My *condition*," Dr. Onyx says forcefully, "does not impact my qualifications, or my duty as chief scientist to be a voice of caution. I do agree that the captain would have grounds to proceed with a landing party, but I stand by my assessment. And I'll thank you not to use my pregnancy as an excuse to question my ability to advise."

I cough to cover a snort of laughter at the flustered look on Dutta's face. Onyx glances at me in annoyance, and I return to the agenda.

"Thank you all for your reports and . . . opinions. Taking all this into consideration, I do intend to proceed with dispatching a landing party. We depart at the beginning of the next cycle. Dutta, select your landing party and have your recommended crew list to me by the end of the day. Onyx, I'll need your recommendations for the science team. We'll reconvene tomorrow to begin working out the details. Is there anything else? You are dismissed."

The crew gathers their devices and files out of the room, Dutta more quickly than the rest. Onyx is the last to leave.

"Onyx, a moment?" She stops halfway out the door and turns to me, arching an eyebrow.

"Yes, Captain?" Her face flushes.

"Go see distribution and get a better-fitting uniform. I'd hate to have to write you up for breach of protocol."

"And what section of the manual am I violating, exactly?" Her eyes flash with defiance.

"Section 8, subsection D: all crew shall be attired in properly-fitted uniforms."

Onyx glares at me. "I'll get right on that, *Captain*. Did you want that before or after my recommendations of the science personnel for the landing party?" She takes a step toward me.

"As long as both are taken care of by the end of the day, Doctor."

She steps even closer to me, until we are toe to toe. I can feel the warmth of her breath on my face. Her eyes are sparkling as she looks up at me.

"Am I dismissed?" she asks softly.

"Until this evening," I reply. "I'll see you in my quarters tonight."

"With pleasure, *Captain*." As she turns to leave, I catch her hand. She turns quickly and I wrap my arms around her.

"*Baby*," I sigh.

"My love," she whispers as she leans against me.

"See you tonight?" I ask, kissing the top of her head and reaching a hand down to stroke her belly.

"I can't wait!" She smiles up at me, kisses me quickly, then heads for the door. I admire her ass as she goes. She has always had a nice ass, but it's somehow *more* during her pregnancy.

"Captain . . ." I hear the smile in her voice. "I can *feel* your eyes on my ass."

I'm setting the table for dinner when I hear the electronic swish of the door opening behind me. It can only be my wife. Dr. Rin Onyx. The most beautiful woman in the galaxy.

"Hi Baby, the meal printer is just about finished printing dinner . . ."

"Take off your pants, and get in bed," Rin orders. I put down the chopsticks and turn around, surprised.

"Baby, sit down, let me get you dinner, and then . . ."

"I said—" She lowers her voice as she begins to unbutton her shirt. "Get. in. bed."

"Sustenance printing: complete," the pleasant automated voice from the printer calls, "Switching to: keep warm mode."

"Are you *sure* you shouldn't eat first?" I fret as I climb onto our bed, which is just offset from our kitchen area. "The doctor said you need to—"

"The only doctor you should be listening to right now, *Captain*," she says severely as she reaches into a compartment, pulling out a handful of silk, "is *me*."

I obediently pull off my pants and center myself on the bed, still worrying about her blood sugar and if her feet are swollen from standing all day. Can I convince her to spend our water allotment on a bath this weekend . . . ?

"Lie down," my goddess of a wife commands. The worries of the day leave my mind as I obediently lie back.

"Hands above your head." I reach up, and she climbs onto me, straddling me. She leans over my face to tie my wrists together with a blue silk scarf, securing them to the slats of the headboard. Her belly presses against my breasts while she works, and I lift my head to kiss her there. When she finishes, she leans down to kiss my forehead, my cheek, my lips.

"You promise you feel up for this?" I whisper.

"I *promise*, my love." She smiles down at me, and I relax into my restraints. Maybe she needs to relieve some tension as much as I do. From her perch, she works the clasps on the front of my shirt, letting it fall open. She skims her fingers across my chest, stopping to tug teasingly at my binder, and then continuing along my collarbone and up my neck. Her hand rests there gently, and she lightly squeezes. The pressure sends my pulse racing, my face flushing hot. I squirm beneath her.

"Is this all right?" she whispers in my ear, nipping gently. I quiver at the sound of her voice, low in my ear, her breath warm and familiar.

"Yes," I reply, trembling beneath her. Her fingers skim along my arms, stretched above my head, my wrists crossed beneath the silk restraint. Every touch feels amplified, my skin more sensitive in my prone state. I *want* to reach out and touch her, to rub my thumb across her cheek, bury my fingers in her hair, sit up and kiss her gorgeous belly; but I can't, and the forced stillness is making me vibrate with excitement.

Rin climbs off me, and slowly removes her shirt, her eyes on mine all the while. I drink in the sight of her: her belly so round and firm and delicious, her breasts straining against her bra. She pulls that off next, and I moan at the sight of her breasts, fuller and heavier in pregnancy.

"*Baby*," I beg as she touches herself, palming her breasts, pinching her own nipples. "*Please* let me touch you. *Please*."

"Patience, *Captain*," she says, smiling as she shimmies out of her pants and panties. I groan at the first glimpse of her mound, so soft and kissable, my mouth watering immediately. She climbs back on top of me, and begins undoing the clasps on the front of my binder. Her fingers are elegant and quick, and then my breasts are free, the cool air perking my nipples.

"*There* you are," she whispers, palming my breasts roughly, and then she pinches both of my nipples. I gasp, my hips trying to rise off the bed, pinned by her weight.

"*That's my girl,*" she coos, watching my face with satisfaction.

"Do you want me to fuck you?" she asks as she runs her hands along my collarbones, then up and down my neck, stopping to squeeze my throat.

"Yes," I gasp, jerking beneath her, warmth pooling between my legs.

"Yes, *what,*" she murmurs.

"*Please,*" I beg. "Please fuck me. *Please.*" I'm panting with anticipation, my wife looking like Mother Earth herself astride me, powerful and in control, and I'm vulnerable and willing beneath her.

"That's a good girl," she coos, taking my chin in her hand. "Open up." I open and she puts three of her fingers in my mouth. "*Such* a *good girl,*" she purrs as I run my tongue up and down her fingers, between them, sucking greedily.

She pulls them out, and moves down, spreading my legs with her knee. I open for her, and whimper as she pulls my panties to the side and slowly enters me.

"*Baby,*" I gasp, jerking desperately against my restraints.

"Mmm, you feel *perfect,*" she groans as she pulls her fingers out, then thrusts into me again. Her other hand rests flat on my lower belly, pushing me down on the bed while her fingers fuck me. She looks like an absolute goddess, resting on her heels between my legs, her fingers inside me. Her face is attentive, rapt as she watches me closely. I want to watch her, but she begins to turn her hand, twisting her fingers inside me; and I lose all thought, gasping, my hips thrusting up to meet her.

"God, baby, *yes*," I groan, "Harder. *Please.*"

"Oh I know what you want, *Captain*." She smiles at me and thrusts harder, quicker, her strokes so familiar, so perfect. I feel my pleasure growing, building, the wet sounds of our joining growing louder.

"Yes, baby, *yes*," I pant, "God, *yes*, I'm gonna . . . *yes!*" I throw my head back as I come, drowning in bliss. Rin strokes me through my orgasm, leaning over me to kiss my cheeks, my lips, my neck . . . whispering all the while, "Yes, my *beautiful* girl. My darling wife. *Yes,* my love."

As my panting slows, I feel her breast against my cheek. She guides her nipple to my mouth. "Suck me, my love," she commands gently. I open my mouth eagerly and take her in, running my tongue over the delicious bud of her nipple, her breast so full and soft and warm against my face. She moans, high and quiet, my favorite sound in the world. Then she grabs my head and pulls me hard against her. I can barely breathe, in utter bliss as she uses my mouth for her pleasure.

I feel her reach up to untie my wrists, and then my arms are free, my hands fervently caressing the soft skin of her back, tangling in her hair, gripping her ass. I flip her gently onto her back, kissing my way down her throat, across her freckled shoulders, before returning my attention to her glorious breasts.

"Tell me what you want," I murmur, and she pauses in her whimpering to guide my head down.

"You know what I want," she says, low and breathy, her hands firm on my head.

"Yes, my goddess," I breathe, nuzzling my face in between her legs, breathing deeply of her scent, her essence, before gently kissing the lips of her pussy. Her skin is so silky soft here: dusky brown with a sweet pink center. I ease my tongue between her folds, loving her soft blissful sigh as I find her clit. My hands spread lovingly around her belly, so round and firm, her stretch marks silky riverbeds beneath my fingers.

Still holding my head, she begins to grind against my face, and I relish the pressure, leaning against her, enjoying her every taste and texture against my tongue, my lips, my face. I reach my arms around her thighs and hug her body to me as I settle in on my belly, my eyes closed, my mouth open, stroking her slowly with my tongue. I trace circles around her clit, then suck gently, loving the feel of her against my lips. I nip her so, so gently and delight in her gasp of pleasure. I nuzzle deeper and work my lips and tongue at her entrance, stroking, tasting, savoring her. Her thrusts against my face grow more rhythmic, and I growl against her, delighting in our perfect, most intimate connection.

As I feel her nearing her climax, I move my attention to her clit, and slide a finger into her wetness, feeling for the spot I know I she loves. I slide a second finger in, and she continues to fuck my face, groaning, gasping, calling my name desperately. I curl my fingers, working patiently as her thrusts grow wilder, more desperate. I work my face from side to side, her clit against my tongue as her fingers pull at my hair until she finally goes silent in ecstasy, her hips thrusting erratically. I move with desperation now, pulling her through until she gasps, pushing my head away.

"God!" she laughs, "You are fucking *amazing!*"

"Switching to: keep cold mode!" The sustenance printer announces cheerily.

"God, I'm starving," Rin says, struggling to sit up. I bring her our meal, and watch her eat. Her hair is a gorgeous mess, her face flushed, eyes bright. She's still naked, her breasts resting gently on her belly, and I rub her foot as she eats, relishing the warm comfort of the moment.

"Aren't you going to eat?" she asks, lifting some steaming greens from her tray.

"Oh, I just did," I smirk. "But when you're done with that . . . I'd love some dessert."

SEVEN

Two of Cups

by Mary Helen Gallucci

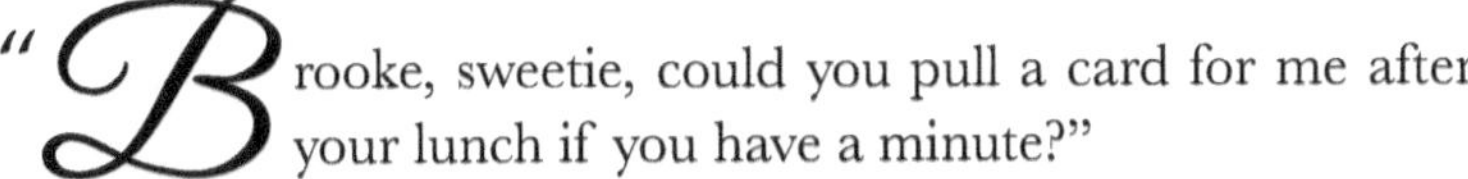

"**B**rooke, sweetie, could you pull a card for me after your lunch if you have a minute?"

"Sure, what's up?" I don't look up from my salmon, sizzling on the stove; but the clatter of my roommate returning to our apartment and kicking her boots off after her early shift is a welcome, familiar sound.

"Just kind of buzzy in the brain, you know how it goes, right? No big deal if you're in the middle of stuff—"

"No no I'm on it! My next consult actually canceled; gimme like, five minutes so I don't burn this—you can have some if you want? Salad? With salmon?—and then I'm all yours."

"Oh my god is that the Long Email Guy wasting your time *again*?! You're charging him by the word at this point, right? AND the full canceled hour; I am rewriting your contract."

It makes my heart swell that she remembers my schedule like this. It's true: this guy has been a pain in my ass; and her declaration of willingness to stand up for me feels so good, even if just a pipe dream. "For real, please. I'd do it, but I'd have to, like—confront him. And I don't want to lose clients."

"Listen, you won't, you're the literal best and I promise not to murder him. Just scare him into paying you what you're worth. Jesus CHRIST that smells good. What do *I* owe you for this divine lunch, and divination?"

"I'll add it to your tab," I say, smirking in an effort to hide my delight. I love sharing with Jenna—my space, my time, my food . . . I'd share anything with her, really. Usually she's the one harping on me about upholding my boundaries—something I appreciate—but I don't really know where to put them with her. Never have.

Jenna pads up behind me in her socks, and gives me a hug around my middle. I tip my head back against hers, just for a second, before she's off. "Okay, lemme quick hop in the shower so I don't get grease on stuff—go ahead and start without me, I'll join you."

I turn off the stove and slide the salmon off my spatula atop the bowls of spinach and veggies I'd prepared. I'd have put the second bowl in the fridge and called it "leftovers" if she hadn't been home for it, but I always secretly hope she will be, and prepare accordingly.

She'd said to start without her, so I sit down with my bowl at our little kitchen table. The sun is pouring through the beads hung in our window, casting rainbows around the room —on the little mushroom lampshade in the corner, on the salmon in my bowl that's now luminescent in the light, on the woo-woo magazine Jenna had picked up for the horoscopes and left open on the table . . .

As much as I enjoy pulling tarot cards now and then, for me it's about the thrill of the symbolism, of finding what new connections my brain might make from the nudge. It makes me a decent reader for them, I think. But Jenna—she's on top of her astrology in a way I could never be. The little rainbow catches my eye, glowing at the center of the circle she's made in purple highlighter around her weekly horoscope.

It feels a little nosy, but the shower is still running . . . surely I have one more minute to myself. I turn the magazine so I can read what she's circled.

> *SCORPIO: week of January 15-21*
> *The last few weeks have been a time of reflection, of honing your priorities; by now you think you know what you want, but a sign this week will help you move forward with clarity. Don't hesitate to ask the universe for more directions when following the map of your heart! She's already on your side and eager to help.*

That last line . . . the first thought that inexplicably slips into my mind is: *I* am *on her side and eager to help!* And then I'm taken aback; I am not *the universe*, what a silly bit to relate to.

But . . . she *did* ask me for help. The tarot reading. And if there's one nudge I'd love to give her heart . . . I *am* kind of empowered to do it. I could stack "The Lovers" card and just hope against hope she might take the hint and give me a chance? What if I'm somewhere, in a private little corner, on that map of her heart? What if I could steer her toward me, today—right now—finally—and it was *real* and she could be in my arms, her lips . . . and mine . . .

The world tilts abruptly as I realize what I'm considering. I wouldn't—*couldn't* dare do such a thing!! Right?! That would be so—*manipulative*, to cheat a system she's put faith in, and entrusted to me?! I can't believe I've just let my mind unspool so far down that path. What good would it do either of us if I finally won her only by forfeiting any right to her trust?

I stab my spinach, and shove a huge forkful into my mouth, chewing aggressively enough that the crunching at least half drowns out my appalled internal monologue.

"Brooke? You good?" Jenna's voice snaps me out of my head, and she slides into the chair across from me, her hair twisted into one of her orange bath towels. One dark lock has escaped, and it brushes against her neck as she pulls her chair closer. I envy it. My heart burns. My lips tingle with the desire to sweep that lock aside and—

"Hey, did yours give you a death threat or something?" Jenna's noticed I've taken her horoscopes. God, was my whole illicit scheme written all over my face?

"No! No, I was just—thinking about something else. You know—Long Email Guy."

"Fucking Long Email Guy. Fuck him."

"Fuck him. . . . Not literally."

"Oh my god no. You're *way* too good for him."

My face flushes, and I stand abruptly. "Anyway, let me grab my cards. Do you want a full spread? Or have a question in mind for them?"

"Oh . . . yeah," Jenna's voice sounds a little distant as I head to the other room. "I think it can be quick? It's not really . . . you know, specific, I just need a nudge, you know? Or—or not."

A nudge. Is this about that horoscope? What is even up in the air in Jenna's life? Her work's been pretty solid—she just got promoted to manager—and as far as I know she hasn't been seeing anyone for more than casual drinks since she broke up with Brad a few months ago. There's this frustrating glow of hope that keeps rising at the edges of my awareness, and I shake my head to shove it down. "Okay, cool. Just life in general."

Is *she* blushing?? "No, there's a—thing, maybe, I don't know. It's fine, let's just see what comes up."

I sit back down and start to shuffle. I can't read Jenna's face—and it's distracting anyway, so I close my eyes and feel the stiff cards sliding against each other, heavy. If she's not asking the question of them, can I? It feels almost like a prayer —one my mom would never approve of—as my fingertips sense the cards slipping by and my mind pleads: *please.*

The cards feel good. Warm. I give them a rub with my thumbs, and then pass the deck to her, my long fingers brushing her wrist as she accepts them. Shit, did I give her a static shock? I'm wearing a wool sweater, the furnace has been running; I feel flooded with embarrassment, for some reason. "Sorry!" I mumble. She gives me a puzzled glance before closing her eyes and beginning her shuffle.

It's only a moment before a card lands on the table. Jenna opens her eyes, sets the deck aside, and, with bated breath, I flip it over.

The card has artwork of a girl in a flowy dress, viewed from the back; her arms are spread, and she's almost floating. Its label says: "The Fool." I'm puzzled for a moment. I'd hoped for something explosive like "The Lovers," and half expected a card with daggers or something that suggested "cut and run!" But this? I glance up at Jenna, and she looks as confused as I am.

I open my guidebook. I'm no expert seer, just a casual girl with a deck; and I don't have this deck and its significance memorized, by any means. "Huh," I say, skimming the text there.

"What is it?" She laughs, hesitantly. "Am I being stupid, should I just . . . forget this whole thing?"

"No, no—" I push the book to her. "It says . . . this is a new beginning? For whatever it is you're . . . worried about?

You're innocent and optimistic and it's perfect for a new journey, I guess." I point to a line and read: "'You may not feel ready, but there is magic in the air. Trust your intuition.'"

Jenna looks up at me, straight into my eyes. Hers are sharp and gray, electric in the afternoon sun. I feel my heart skip a beat, and I swallow it down before it lodges in my throat. Then she squints. "Do another? Just . . . to be sure. I feel like the next one is the one."

"Oh—yeah, sure." I snatch the deck back and close my eyes. Then I take a deep breath, and start to shuffle." *It's totally fine*, I think at the cards, trying to drown out the pounding of my heart in my head. *Say whatever you want. Whatever the right thing is. It's all good, forget I asked, never mind.*

I need to pass her the cards before she can tell how flustered I'm getting, but I can't bear to touch her again so I set the deck on the table and slide it over.

This time, it feels like she shuffles forever. I keep my eyes closed, focusing on my breathing and the swish-clack of the stiff cards in her hands until she says, "Okay, got it."

We open our eyes. There's a card between us, and I flip it. Then I blink. The illustration is two hands, intertwined, with a kind of electric aura around them. It's—*us. Oh my god universe, I said 'never mind!!'* It's Two of Cups, and I know what that means, but, hedging, I start to flip through the book. "Oh— two of cups, that's—a really gentle one, water, emotions . . ."

"Soulmates," says Jenna. I meet her eyes and they're on fire. "It's the friends-to-lovers trope on a fucking card."

"I mean—" I start, but I can't look away from her face, and it's like her eyes are growing, looming toward me, devouring me as my heart races out of control. "The book says it's just—" I glance at it. "Just whispers of—romance, and attraction, and"—I have to look up again, her face is too magnetic—"and b-bliss . . ."

"Oh shit," Jenna says, jumping up, "That salmon is getting cold!" She grabs her bowl from where I'd left it next to the stove, and then leans there, sinking back on an elbow, aggressively casual. "Ohw, my gawd!" She's shoved in a giant forkful, chewing messily. "Thish is fucking *delischious!* Thanks sho much for the reading, babe!" She laughs, and it's a forced wheeze through the greens. "I know you think this schtuff is schtupid, thanksh for humoring me!"

I blink at her. "I—I don't think it's *stupid*, I just—"

"No no you're totally right dude, it'sh shilly."

". . . Okay." Suddenly I feel like I can't be in this room anymore. I stick what's left of my salad in the fridge as I pass it on my way out. "I gotta . . . go . . . y'know, stuff."

I'm sitting on my bed, staring at my phone. There's really no telling how much time has passed since that—whatever it was in the kitchen—because I've dissociated a little, trying to distract myself by scrolling through reels and cat videos. It's not working. I'm stuck on Jenna, because—what the *fuck* was *that??*

Finally growing annoyed with my own looping thoughts, I open my texts. There's one from Jenna, sent an hour ago: "Hey babe! On my way home, can we talk?"

Can we talk?? I must have missed it while cooking. Did she think *that* was the "talk?" Um, no—that was not a "talk," that was something that demands even more of a talk to disentangle, because now that I'm back on this I feel like my insides are crawling. I need to do something. Urgently.

Hey, I type, *sorry I missed this!*

My thumb hits "send" automatically, before I can consider that I've just started a ball rolling that I'm not sure I have the willpower to stop.

I continue: *Yeah, I want to talk, too.*

Send. She apparently isn't on her phone reading this in real time, so I barrel ahead.

I don't know if this is what's going on with you—it seems like there's something up—but

I hesitate. Nothing I've said is a commitment yet. This could still be about anything. I hit send.

I love you

I huff a laugh while I backspace.

I don't know if any of your weirdness is about me?

Backspace.

What's up with me, is . . .

Delete. Then I just—type it:

I think I might be in love with you

—And send. There. It's done! It's almost a relief. My skin stops crawling while a new kind of sinking dread sets in. I push on.

I think it's possible that's your deal too? But if not I'm so sorry, please still be my friend, I swear I can still be cool it's no big deal

Send. . . . I should leave it there, stop my nervous rambling and let her answer so I don't dig my humiliating hole deeper, but I just *need* to contextualize, to explain myself just in case— in *case* . . .

Like, I know you just said tarot was stupid and I know that's normally my stance too, but maybe this *is the nudge?*

Send.

For both of us?

Send. Then I double-tap and delete that last one. She still hasn't read any of this, according to my phone. Am I being incredibly presumptuous?? I don't know if I'm *right* or if I'm just hurdling further and further into left field . . .

Anyway I just—think you're incredible, the most beautiful person I've ever known

Send.

Inside and out

Send.

*And I love being around you and I just want to be around you, like, *all the time**

Send.

I mean, I know we're already roommates but if you wanted to be . . . closer

Send.

Physically

Send—delete, oh my god.

Please tell me?

Send.

I wait. My heart is pounding and I scroll up to reread my blather, mortified and also . . . maybe a little proud? I'm finally just being real and open, addressing my feelings with honesty and opening up the possibility that *maybe—*

The "read" receipt appears.

Oh god. My stomach drops. I immediately start typing furiously, my thumbs flying.

Seriously tho if this is weird please PLEASE disregard, like this never happened oh my god

There's a knock at my door.

"Y-yeah?" I choke.

The door flies open to reveal Jenna in motion: as soon as I blink, she's crawling onto my bed. She climbs right onto my lap, taking my face in her hands and—oh my god she's kissing me. Her lips are so soft—*so soft*, and warm, and she tastes *incredible.* Her fingertips are delicate chilly bursts of sensation at my jaw and cheeks and she's pressing into me, my back against the pillows and god—*god* does this mean it's *real?* I wasn't dumb or wishful thinking or bursting our friendship I was—*right??* Because nothing has ever felt more right than this moment.

"Jenna—" I gasp between fervent kisses, "What—ahhhh —" She's taken the moment to move down my neck, and my pulse has gone haywire. I want to rip her clothes off—I want to rip *mine* off, just expose my whole self to her if *this* is the reception I get for opening up. Maybe pull my skin off, too, and just hand over my whole galloping heart to her like *please take me, I'm yours.*

"Is this okay?" she pants between kisses, and when I groan in affirmation she nips at my throat with her teeth before soothing the spot with her hot tongue. My hands are in her hair—it's still hanging in damp curls from her shower, curtaining her face, and I scoop it back to see her as she slowly descends my body.

The sight takes my breath away: her gorgeous face, all perfect curves and arches, as familiar to me as my own—but at a brand-new angle, looking up at me through her lashes, and beaming like all the awe and wonder and exhilaration I'm feeling are reflected through a mirror.

"I'm gonna—devour you, Brooke, if you don't stop me." Her voice is dripping with passion and I realize abruptly that *I'm* fucking dripping, too. Every nerve ending is humming as she skims her hands under my shirt, waiting for my permission.

"*Please,*" I plead. "Jenna, I've—*wanted* this, wanted *you,* but I wasn't sure—"

"GOD," she growls, "me too."

"Please," I say again, whimpering as she rucks my shirt up and over my chest. She sighs heavily and glances at my face before curling her fingers around the top edges of my bra cups and pulling them down together.

"*FUCK,*" she cries, staring unabashedly at my breasts, my nipples puckering rapidly from the exposure, "*FUUUCK,* Brooke, oh my god *FUCK—ME—SIDEWAYS,* you are— FUCKING GLORIOUS, *FUCK!!!*"

An uncontrollable laugh bubbles out of me and tears prick my eyes as she practically shouts in her enthusiasm. That's one thing about Jenna that's so beautiful, and that I adore so fully, I've never dared look for words to express it to her: how she jumps with both feet into the deep end every time she gets excited about something.

My laugh chokes off abruptly when I feel her tongue on my nipple. It's hot and slick and then she bites, moaning as she tugs me from side to side like it's everything she's craved in life and she's *digging in.* She releases me and sucks, laving at the bud in her mouth with her tongue, the slender fingers of her other hand groping across my other breast to grasp and pull at that nipple too.

I'm writhing and bucking under her ministrations, pulling away to make her tugging harder, sharper. I can't fucking believe my beautiful goddess Jenna has her mouth on my breast. I can't get enough of the surreal vision and I feel every glance, every tug, running new electric lines that light up my clit.

The sensation builds until I can't hold in a shriek: "*Jenna!!*" She lifts her head, grinning with all her sparkling white teeth. One dogtooth is a little forward and pointed and it's always squeezed something delicious in me to see it when she smiles. I push up on my elbows to kiss her and relish the thrill that I *can.*

When I drop back I notice that she's not wearing a bra, and the way she's hovering over me, her light oversized shirt droops between us, giving me an expansive view of her cleavage that I've only very guiltily glanced away from before. Now I'm staring—I know it—and she sways a little so I can glimpse the edges of her dark nipples. "Jenna," I whimper, and she takes my hand and guides it to cup her breast through her thin shirt. And Jesus fucking Christ she's *so soft*, and so warm, and she fills my hand like we were made for this fit. I graze my fingertips where the fabric protrudes a bit over the nub of her nipple, and we both gasp. I feel light-headed and I'm not sure if it's because I'm breathing so heavily, or because I'm allowed to just—pull the stretchy material until I can *see* every luscious curve of this girl I've only ever imagined in the privacy of my bedroom, with my vibrator.

I do it. And I see her, and I swallow hard, my pussy melting with liquid heat.

My hips grind against her desperately—I can't stop them —and she growls, dipping to catch my nipple between her teeth again before licking and nipping down my ribs, my belly. Then she pauses, propping her chin on the button of my jeans and meeting my eyes. "Brooke," she rasps, "Can I please fuck you? I really fucking want to, like—*so* goddamn bad, I swear it's all I've thought about for *months*."

"Really?!" I breathe, stunned by this revelation. I give in, finally, to the urge I've been having every day—every moment I've been around her, lately—and brush the pad of my thumb over her eyebrow, her cheekbone, her full lower lip. The caress checks her energy, just a little, and I see it register in the softness of her eyes. She melts into my palm.

"Really," she says, gentler. "I—I'm in love with you too, Brooke. I don't *think* I am, I know it. I just didn't . . . How the hell were you so brave just now?! Who even are you? God, I'm obsessed." She presses her face to the seam between my legs, and inhales deeply. "I can *smell* you," she groans. "Please, let me show you?"

"Show me?"

"That I—love you."

I stroke her hair one more time, then unbutton my jeans and start to edge them down over my hips. "Yes."

"Yeeessssss . . ." Jenna wastes no more time. She helps shuck my pants off, pulling my underwear with them. Then she grips the back of my thigh, just behind my knee, and moves my bent leg up and to the side, giving herself access. I'm so open to her right now, I feel myself flushing everywhere, from my face to my tingling nipples to the swollen folds she's spreading with her fingers. "Brooke," she breathes, "God, babe, you're perfect."

An expression of awe has transformed her face—she's my Jenna but she's *radiant* and I can't believe this is happening. It's beyond my wildest fantasy and I'd had no idea she could *glow* like this. I need a pinch to ground this in reality, I need her to — "Please kiss me?"

Jenna crawls up my body and presses her lips to mine with an unfettered eagerness that makes my heart soar. Her tongue presses into my mouth, sweet and sure, and when her fingers begin stroking between my folds, the sensations melt together until my whole body is floating on a cloud of sheer bliss. I can do nothing but feel—my own gasps and whimpers are distant background noise—and it's *Jenna*, and she wants me, and I'm hers.

It's maybe been a minute or an hour when her voice breathes low and hot in my ear: "Can I put a finger in you, babe?"

My lip is between my teeth as I'm yearning, pressing myself into her hand. "Mmmmmhmmm."

She closes her eyes and exhales, low and guttural, as she

sinks into me, and I can't believe I ever *didn't* know this feeling of her, deep inside me. "God, Brooke," she groans, moving and pressing, exploring me. "I've thought about doing this every night—hell, every time I have half a second at work—fuck—every time I see you on the couch in your fucking flannel pajama pants—fuuuuuuck—"

I cry out, and she does too. Her declaration is too good to be true; it's sending almost unbearable waves of pleasure through me and she's not even finished yet.

"Brooke," she pants, the muscles in her arms flexing, "Every time I touch myself, I want it to be you. I have to whisper your name into my pillow so you don't hear me through the wall, I just—" She adds another finger and I didn't know how desperate I was for it until she's stretching me so exquisitely I might be screaming. "I'm fucking obsessed with you and this feels even better than I imagined, god you're *so perfect.*"

My hips are pressing her harder, begging uncontrollably, and I'm so full of her fingers and her words that when my clit grinds hard against her slick palm I come undone with a cry. Her fingers are there and I'm squeezing her—it's *her*—and this—pulsing around her, my sex in her hand—is exactly, *exactly* the "closeness" with her I'd most deeply desired.

I sigh heavily, dropping to the bed as I come down, reeling. For a moment I'm certain this was all a euphoric dream, and I don't dare open my eyes. But then—Jenna is at my neck again, kissing me; and when I finally, reluctantly, look at her face . . . her eyes are so soft, so radiant, and brimming with unshed tears.

"God, you're so fucking beautiful," she breathes.

"You are," I manage, and cup her cheek in my palm.

Then she pulls her fingers from me—I'd forgotten they weren't just a part of me now, the way we fit together—and, flopping next to me on the bed, she begins to lick those fingers clean almost reverently, like my juices are the best thing she's ever tasted. "Brooke—*fuck*, babe, you taste as good as you smell—even better—fucking *incredible* . . ."

"Is it . . . my turn, Jenna? Can I really touch you?"

She laughs a little incredulously, then languidly pulls off her shirt with an exaggerated stretch. Oh god, she's a vision, her supple skin absolutely luminous in my eyes. I sit up and pull her to me, kissing her, and then cautiously—reverently—taking one of her breasts in my hand. "MMMmmmm," she moans against my mouth; then gently says, "Brooke—just to be up front—"

I quickly start to release her, but she holds me firmly. "No no, please—*please* keep doing this. I just want you to know, I don't think I'm into, like, being penetrated? I just—think I need a break from it or something, after . . . But everything else . . . *everything.* Else." She smirks at me pointedly. "*Please.*"

"Absolutely," I murmur, tucking her words away in my mind to process later, while my heart swells at her vulnerability, confiding this in me. And the way she knows herself—I'm in awe of her. I'm so honored to know this intimate detail about this girl I love—and to have this opportunity to be with her and respect her and give her exactly what she wants? It makes my chest ache for fullness. I want to worship her. "Would you—would you please sit on my face?"

Jenna grins. Then bites her lip. "Yeah, but I have a question first."

"What is it?"

"You stacked that tarot deck, didn't you? You *sneaky* little—"

My mouth drops open. "What?! I would never!!"

"How was it *so* perfect, Brooke? Two of Cups?? Really??

When you're just sitting on a confession like *I love you?* You *had* to know what you were doing!"

"I . . . okay, I thought about it, because I really . . . hoped . . . somewhere deep down you wanted this? And needed a nudge? But I swear I actually didn't."

"Riiight . . ."

"And how could I have? You shuffled them yourself!"

Jenna tips her chin down, squinting suspiciously. "So you're telling me it was 'the universe' pushing us together?"

"I mean . . ." I laugh, and kiss her. "I'm pretty sure it was my texts actually pushing us together. The cards just made things weird for a minute."

"Huh," says Jenna. "Spooky." Then she unties the drawstring on her pants.

EIGHT

The Duet

by Natalie Naudus

’m just dozing off when I hear the front door close.

"Chris? Is that you?" I call sleepily.

"Beth? Babe, why are you still awake?" Chris comes into our bedroom, kicking off her shoes and dropping her keys on the nightstand. She sheds her shirt, pants, and binder, and then climbs into bed, melting into me.

"I just got caught up in this book." I pause to yawn, then continue, "Tell me about your date? How was it?"

"It was ok!" She rests her head on my shoulder. She smells faintly of wine and cream.

"What did you have for dinner?"

"Shrimp Alfredo and white wine. I brought you some garlic bread."

"Oh yeah?" I perk up.

"Do you want it now?" She laughs, "I thought you'd be asleep!"

"I'm always up for a late night snack! I'll go warm it up, and then you tell me about your date."

"Perfect!"

. . .

I unwrap the foil packet in the kitchen, and slide the bread into the toaster. Its internal timer clicks quietly as I hear the shower turn on, and Chris's resonant humming emanates from the bathroom. I pour myself a glass of red, and check my dating app matches while I wait. I respond to a message from someone I've been chatting with on and off, and then open my conversation with Sam. She wants to meet.

"How's next Tuesday?" she writes. "I'll make you dinner!"

I check the calendar. Chris is out of town at a work conference next week. It's perfect timing. We don't always schedule our dates while the other is busy, but it's nice when it works that way. Dinner at Sam's place, though . . . If she were a man, I'd insist on a public restaurant. But we've been chatting for a week, and she seems harmless.

"Sure!" I type. "Let me know what I can bring!"

The toaster dings and I pull the bread out and onto a plate, then head to the bedroom. Chris is towel-drying her short-buzzed hair, all cozy in her flannel pajama pants and baggy t-shirt. She climbs into bed and reaches for the wine.

"Hey, I poured for one!" I laugh.

"Better grab the bottle then!" She smirks at me over the rim. I retrieve the bottle, and cozy up in bed with her.

"So, tell me about it?" I say, taking a bite of the crispy buttery bread. "Mmmmm," I moan around it. "So good!"

She smiles at my enjoyment and reaches up to tuck a wisp of graying hair behind my ear. "It was alright! She wasn't really what I expected from our text conversations? A bit self-absorbed, I guess? I didn't *dislike* her, but I don't know that we had a real connection."

"Ah, too bad." I take another bite. She leans toward me

and I feed her a bite as well. She snuggles into me in the comfy quiet. She's so cute, my tough masc wife, all cozied up against me like the sweetheart she is. "I'm meeting up with Sam next week—that librarian I've been talking to?"

"Wasn't she really young?" Chris sips our wine.

"Compared to *us*, yes." I kiss her forehead.

"How old is she again?"

"Twenty-four, I think?"

"So that's . . . what is it . . ."

"A twenty-one-year difference," I supply.

"Hey, I was getting there," she huffs with fake annoyance. I chuckle and kiss her fondly. She hands me the wine. "Here, take a sip."

When I finish, she takes the glass and plate from me, placing them on the nightstand. "Take off your clothes, cradle-robber."

"Woah, are we doing this?" I laugh. "I just ate garlic bread . . ."

"Why do you think I had a bite? Now I taste it too. It cancels out your garlic breath."

"*Our* garlic breath!" I laugh, and she winds her arms around me and kisses me.

"What do you want, baby?" I whisper in her ear as she writhes gently against me.

"You," she replies, climbing on top of me. I slip my hands beneath her faded tee and feel her skin, so warm and plush, every fold and valley perfect and luscious. I take her shirt off, and she helps me out of my sleep clothes. Then she reaches into the nightstand drawer. "I want to fuck you," she says simply, climbing off me to pull on her harness.

She holds my gaze when she enters me, her eyes loving

and hungry. I reach down and play with my clit as she thrusts into me, the length of her delicious. She kisses my neck, answering my moans with groans of her own. Sweat gathers in her short hair from her exertion as she changes her strokes: first slow and languid, then firm and deep. I feel my pleasure building, mounting as she leans over me, her breast in my face.

"Beth," she gasps, "suck me. Pinch me, baby. I know you are close . . ."

Her breast fills my mouth, smothering my face. I can barely breathe around her, and I am in absolute ecstasy. I reach for her other nipple, tugging it while I suck on her, and she thrusts into me as we come undone together.

Sam answers the door in dark jeans and a dress shirt that's buttoned to the top. She has short, bleached-blonde hair, and god, she's even younger than I imagined.

"Beth?"

"Sam! So nice to meet you! I brought a bottle of red . . ."

"Beautiful! Come on in!"

Her apartment is cozy—nicer than I expected for someone in their 20s—but it still feels youthful to me; Chris' decorating style veers strongly toward Tenured Lesbian Professor. The table is set nicely, candles are lit, and soft music is playing from a Bluetooth speaker.

"What a beautiful apartment!" I say, looking around. "Oh, are you a musician?" I gesture toward the keyboard and cello by the couch.

"I wish!" Sam says, leading me into the kitchen. "It's my

roommate's. Actually, they're touring with a production of Evita right now. They take a lot of out-of-town gigs."

"Ah, I see! Can I help with anything?"

"Pour us some wine?" Sam hands me a bottle opener. Her hands are tattooed with elegant foliage that disappears under the cuff of her sleeves. A hot tattooed librarian? Yes please.

"So I assume they don't play the cello, unless that's a spare?" I ask as I uncork the bottle, pouring us each a glass.

"Yeah, they're a violinist! It's fantastic hearing them practice, or teach a lesson here on occasion. It really makes me wish I'd stuck with my own studies."

"Oh, what instrument did you play?"

"I took piano lessons when I was a kid, from this grouchy old man. But a few times, when he was out of town, this *beautiful* woman, another teacher at the studio, would sub for him. To be honest, I had a huge crush on her. She was a pretty big part of my Queer awakening."

"I think a lot of Queer women have similar stories! Falling in love with a teacher seems to be a rite of passage!"

I look at the pictures on the refrigerator as I sip my wine, pausing to examine one in particular more closely. It's an Asian man and woman with a little girl, her hair long and her dress pink and frilly. I squint, lowering my glasses to see better at close range. "Is this your family?"

Sam glances at the photo as she reaches around me to open the fridge. She rests her hand low on my back as she does so, and I feel a tingle of interest. She's very attractive.

"Oh yeah, that's my parents and me. We used to go to that fair every year." Sam returns to the stove, and I look closer at the picture.

"You look so familiar, I . . ." And then it dawns on me. "Samantha?!"

Sam looks up from the stove. "I mean, yeah, I used to go by Samantha when I was younger . . ."

"Where did you take piano lessons?" I ask, excitement rising in my voice.

"Um . . . at a local music store, I think?"

"Music and Arts in Fairbanks?"

"I think so?"

"Sam. I think . . . I taught at that studio . . . Did I teach you a few lessons?"

Sam abandons the stove. "Miss Bethany?!" We are laughing and gasping in shock and delight. "You didn't say anything about being a piano teacher!" Sam accuses, laughing.

"I haven't taught in years! I got a Masters in administration and got a position at the Lindhurst Art Museum. That's why I quit teaching—and where I met my wife, incidentally! But *you*"—I glare at her. "You really didn't recognize me? Have I changed that much?"

"I was eight when you left; you seemed so . . . tall and unreachable to me then! I thought something was familiar about you, but I never dreamed . . ." Sam runs a hand through her hair, laughing in disbelief.

"Well, this is quite the turn of events!" I wipe tears from my eyes. "Wait. Now I know you had a *crush* on me."

"Ms. Bethan—"

"Please," I interrupt. "Just keep calling me Beth."

"Beth." Sam smiles. "I don't think that crush ever went away. You are . . . so beautiful."

I flush with pleasure. "You grew up awfully attractive yourself! So tell me how you ended up—"

"Fuck! My risotto!" Sam turns to the stove, stirring desperately. "Aw hell, it's ruined!"

. . .

Thirty minutes later we are laughing on the living room rug, drinking wine and eating pizza. It feels like catching up with an old friend, but with the sizzling new relationship energy of a budding connection.

"Well, Sam," I laugh, "to be honest, I was fully intending to fuck you when you opened the door, but now I'm not sure I should!"

"Why not?"

"Because you were a student I taught!"

"Hardly," Sam insists. "Only those few times grouchy Mr. Albertson was out of town, and you were never anything but completely professional!"

"As long as we can both agree that there is nothing untoward happening here!" I laugh.

"Did you . . . mean that, though? About when I opened the door?" Sam asks, looking pleased with herself.

I reach out and touch her chin with a single finger. "You are *very* attractive, Sam."

Sam rises abruptly, goes to the keyboard and sits on the bench. "I wonder if I can remember it . . ." Haltingly, she picks out the tune to an early primer piece.

"No!" I laugh. But she keeps going. Slowly but surely, she's remembering it. I rise to join her, placing my glass of wine on the coffee table. Sliding on the bench next to her, my hip snug against hers, I improvise a simple Alberti bass accompaniment. We finish with a flourish, laughing, and turn toward each other. My laughter dies when Sam reaches out her tattooed fingers and gently touches my chin.

"Is this ok?" she asks softly.

"Yes," I breathe.

She leans in and kisses me, her strong fingers traveling down my throat. She holds my jaw firmly and moves to kiss below my ear. As she does, she whispers, "I would very much like to fuck you now, if you don't mind."

She stands and pulls me to my feet, leading me into her bedroom. There, she shuts the door and pushes me onto her bed, kneeling in front of me. She kisses my knee, and slowly works her way down my calf, and back up again, her kisses slow and deep.

"Where do you get the confidence . . ." I shudder a little, "To touch me like this?"

Sam pauses in her ministrations. "I may be young . . ." She slides her hand up my skirt, gripping my hip with strong fingers. "But I'm a good learner. What do you like, Beth?"

"Why don't you warm me up and I'll let you know."

"I can do that." Sam moves her hand between my legs, cupping me, pressing her palm firmly against my sex. She lifts my shirt with her other hand and pulls down the cup of my bra, leaning in to breathe warmly on my nipple. Slowly, deliberately, she takes my nipple between her teeth, pricking it gently with her incisors. I gasp, and her eyes fly up to meet mine. This image—her before me, grinning with my nipple between her teeth—shakes loose the last of my inhibitions, and I grip her head and press her face against my breast. She groans and grinds her palm against my mound more firmly, and I can feel my wetness growing.

I feel her fingers pull aside the fabric of my panties and gently trace my slit, drawing the moisture there up toward my clit. I sigh and drop my head back, and there she is—kissing my neck, gently biting, groaning with a sexy, throaty sound that I'm quickly growing to love—as her fingers continue to explore my sex.

"Get on the bed, on your hands and knees," she whispers in my ear. I obey, pulling my shirt off as I reposition. One of my breasts is still out, where she'd freed it from my bra. She reaches one strong, tattooed arm around me and grips my breast, while with her other hand she reaches up my skirt, pushes aside my panties and slides a finger inside me. I am exposed, and wet, and she's holding me steady, my mostly-clothed state heightening my arousal.

"Is this all right?" she asks, low in my ear, and I nod.

"God, you . . . feel so good," I gasp. "Give me another finger?" Her hand appears in front of me, and I obediently take two of her fingers into my mouth, tasting my own juices, sliding my tongue between her fingers and around them. And then her hand is back between my legs, thrusting into me, my panties pulled tight and to the side. I feel her hips bucking against my ass as she continues to fuck me.

When she pulls out, I feel the loss keenly.

"Let's get the rest of these clothes off you." She unclasps my bra. I remove it, toss it to the side, and then shimmy out of my skirt and panties. She waits until I'm watching her, and then begins unbuttoning her shirt, starting at the very top. Her tattooed fingers are deft and efficient, and my mouth waters as more and more of her skin becomes visible. She tosses her shirt over a chair and removes her pants, and then her black boxers and sports bra. Her breasts are small and beautiful; her nipples look dark and delicious.

"*Please* let me touch you," I beg, and she nods. I stand and kiss her hard, backing her up against the wall. Her mouth is so soft, her teeth slick beneath my tongue. I take her hands and hold them above her, restraining her. She tilts her head back, exposing her throat to me, and I kiss her there hungrily, moving lower to nip at her delicate collarbones.

Then I let her hands go and move to her breasts, circling one nipple with my tongue while squeezing the other with my hand. Her nipple is delicious and I savor the feel of it in my mouth, squeezing it steadily between my tongue and my palate. She whimpers and I fall to my knees, breathing deeply of her scent as I admire her sex. Her folds are dark and brown, with wetness coating the edges . . . and as I spread her, I see the brilliant pink of her revealed. I look up. She is watching me hungrily.

"May I?"

"Please," she begs. "Do you need . . ." She grabs me a pillow, and I put it under my knees before returning my attention to her glistening pussy.

I place my mouth on her, and relish her sharp intake of breath, the demanding feeling of her fingers gripping my hair, pressing my head against her. I slide my tongue between her folds, scooping into her, pulling her flavor—her nectar—into my mouth.

"Fuuuuck," Sam pants. "Beth. Beth. My god. I . . . Fuck . . ."

I smile as I continue, swooping my tongue around her clit, licking up and down, luxuriating in her taste, her smell, her swollen folds against my face.

"Can you . . ." she gasps, "put a finger . . ."

"Wait, do you have a vibrator?" I ask.

"Yeah, in there." She points at the nightstand. I pull one out and hand it to her.

"Use it on yourself," I command.

"Yes, ma'am."

I lean against her, kissing her mouth as she presses the vibrator to her clit. Then I pull back, slipping two fingers in her mouth. Her eyes are glazed with desire as she licks them greedily. Wrapping one hand gently around the base of her jaw, I reach the other down, sliding my fingers inside her. Her legs are trembling, and I can feel her quivering around my fingers.

"Is this ok?" I ask.

"Yes," she shudders. "Fuck, Beth, I'm gonna come, I . . . aaaah—" She cries out as I thrust into her again, fucking her steadily, watching her face—watching her mouth fall slack, her eyes roll back as she gasps, and shakes, and comes around my fingers.

Her wetness is dripping down my hand as I pull out of her. She collapses into my arms, and I lay us out on the bed, kissing her forehead gently while she recovers. When she does, she bounces back up, with all the youthful vigor of a twenty-four-year-old.

"Can I please, *please*, fuck you with my strap-on?"

I smile. "Yes. Yes, you may."

NINE

Prick of Her Teeth

by Natalie Naudus and Mary Helen Gallucci

"**H**ey, do you mind if I come in and brush my teeth?"

"Oh yeah, come on in!" Lilith calls from the shower.

I slip into the steamy bathroom, breathing deeply of the pleasant scents of Lilith's shampoo and soap. Running the tap briefly to wet my toothbrush, I apply toothpaste and then brush my teeth, looking idly around the bathroom. There I am in the mirror, wild sex hair, wearing only a t-shirt. I admire the ornate scrollwork on the wallpaper. Wow, Lilith has like . . . pretty gothic taste.

"You have a chandelier? In your bathroom?" I call over the noise of the running water.

"Oh yeah, I found it thrifting! Cool, isn't it?"

"Yeah!" I reach up and touch it, setting it gently spinning. Then I spit into the sink, and am rinsing when I hear the water shut off and the curtain open. I look up, of course. I mean, I've seen Lil naked, and I just can't get enough. And her, glistening, exiting the shower? I've been looking forward to this moment all evening.

. . . But when I look up into the mirror, I don't see her. "Lil?"

"Yeah?" she answers. I whip around. And there she is, gloriously naked, thin streams of water running down her skin, and I want to stare but . . . but . . . I look back at the mirror. She's not there. I turn again to the shower and there she is, watching me with a smirk on her face.

"Take it easy, darling, you're going to give yourself whiplash."

"But . . . You are there. So . . . so why aren't you . . ." I gesture helplessly to the mirror.

"I'm a vampire, darling."

"I'm sorry, a *what?*"

"A vampire."

"Like . . . a *vampire*-vampire?"

"Drinks blood, avoids the sun, supernatural powers . . . you *have* read Twilight?

"I know what a vampire *is*, I just . . . I mean I didn't . . . I wasn't . . ."

"We've been hanging out for a month, my love. How are you just now noticing?"

"I don't know, I just thought you were cool and quirky and . . . I don't know?!"

"The fact that I wear long sleeves and a sun hat every day?"

"I thought you were passionate about UV protection!"

"The way I eat beef tartare daily?"

"It's a classy fucking food!"

"My allergy to garlic?"

" . . . Okay that one should have tipped me off."

"Clarissa, I had *vampire* in my dating profile!"

"I THOUGHT YOU MEANT LIKE, SPIRITUALLY!"

Lilith laughs, low and throaty, as she grabs a towel and

dries herself off. I look in the mirror. Sure enough, there is the towel, hovering, and rubbing . . . empty space. I can't see her at all. Just the goddamned towel. I watch, mesmerized, as the towel dances and weaves. Returns to the rack. A cold hand touches my shoulder.

"Aah!" I jump, turning to see Lilith grinning at me.

"You didn't wonder why my hands are so cold?"

"I'm always hot, they feel so nice!"

"Oh yeah?" Lilith winds her arms around me, nuzzling into the back of my neck. I relish her touch, and then return my gaze to the mirror. It's so odd *feeling* her, knowing she's there, but not *seeing* her.

Her hands tease the hem of my t-shirt, and then slide under, grazing my skin gently. Her fingers trace my hips, across my belly. I twitch with pleasure.

"Is this ok?"

"Yeah, I mean—we *just* had sex but . . . I've never been touched by an invisible vampire before . . ."

Her hand reaches up the nape of my neck, grabbing my hair and pulling it firmly. I let her, tipping my head back, my neck stretching and lengthening. I swallow hard, my throat looking very . . . *exposed* in the mirror. I feel her fingers trace the column of my neck. They wind feathery circles along my collarbone.

"I can't get enough of your skin," Lilith whispers low in my ear. I shiver, my hips bucking, heat pooling in my sex. "You will taste"—her tongue flicks my ear—"absolutely"— her hand brushes my throat—"delicious"—I'm panting with want, my nipples tight and hard against the fabric of my shirt —". . . running down my throat."

I shudder, this feverish mix of chill and heat bewildering my senses, fogging my brain. I feel her behind me, her hands on me, her breath on my neck; but my reflection is just me. My neck is exposed and my chest is heaving as I pant with arousal, my back arched, hips tilted back towards her.

Then I'm watching as the neckline of my shirt stretches impossibly down, down and to the side until the bud of my nipple pops free, then the round globe of my breast. I hear her growl, feel it hot in my ear. "Look at you," she rasps, low. "Watch."

The bottom hem of my shirt undulates as I feel her cold palm slip across my thigh to my belly, and I shudder, leaning back into her. My shirt rises and I glimpse the lips of my sex between my trembling legs. Then the hem of the shirt falls, but hikes up again as her hands explore me, grazing and pinching and scratching and it feels like she is *everywhere*. When she finally lifts my shirt off entirely, I'm there in the mirror—naked—covered in red markings ranging from faint to angry, and my skin is tingling, humming with sensation. I suddenly realize I'm panting.

"Look at you, so beautiful with my marks all over you," she says, gently fingering the marks on my breasts, my hips.

"When I asked you to . . . bite me before, I didn't realize who I was talking to," I say, trying and failing to steady my voice.

"You don't mind a little pain?" she asks, approval in her tone.

"I—I love it," I confess.

"And do you enjoy watching? Watching yourself flush with pleasure under my touch?"

"Y-yes," is all I can muster, because a firm hand is lifting my knee to rest on the countertop, and I'm impossibly balanced, trusting that my eyes are deceiving me, that she's there at my back. My head swims, but she feels so solid and *supernaturally* strong, gripping me about my middle. My folds, pink and swollen in the mirror, are already spread, but an icy touch spreads them wider; the hood of my clit peels back and it's a pearl glistening in the vanity lights before my eyelids slam closed against the sensation of her fingers fluttering against it. I'm shuddering, moaning, rocking against her, needing more pressure . . .

"Open your eyes and watch," she commands me.

When I obey and look in the mirror, she's there, ready: my opening broadens, gleaming and milky, deep blood red, as I feel her fingers sink deep inside. Then my pussy is rippling, undulating as she pulls out and thrusts in again, faster, harder—and suddenly I'm aware she's nipping at my shoulder, my neck—tiny pinpricks of sensation that can only be her teeth, alternating with the wet relief of her tongue, soothing, broad and soft.

"Lilith," I plead, "Bite me. Please bite me. Please."

"Oh I can do more than that, pet." She halts, pulling out of me, and I squeeze deep and empty at the loss.

"Can you . . ." I swallow. "Drink my blood? Will it hurt me?"

"Oh, on the contrary, darling. Besides the initial prick of my teeth, which I happen to know you enjoy, the bite of a vampire"—her withdrawn fingers now stroke my throat, slick and fragrant, and I feel her shudder with me—"provides great pleasure."

I realize that I'm desperate for her. And I'm suddenly afraid of the choices I'm making in this lustful, foggy state.

"Wait!" I turn around and catch her hands. Her lids are low, her dark gaze heavy with lust.

"What is it, darling?"

"I just . . . Is it safe?"

"Perfectly safe, my love."

"Will there be a wound?"

"No more than the other love marks I've left on you."

"I'm not going to turn into a vampire myself, am I?"

She chuckles, low in her throat. "No, my darling. There's no chance of that." She grazes the underside of my chin with her delicate fingers, gently stroking my face. "But we don't need to, my pet. It's entirely your choice."

And with that freedom to say no, need surges through me. Desperation. "I want you to drink from me."

"You're sure?"

"I'm sure. Take me. Please."

She smiles and kisses me, her lips so soft and cool against my own. Then, firmly, she turns me back towards the mirror. My nipples are tight, my breath growing quick with anticipation. I feel her kiss my back, her arms winding around me as her hands cup my breasts, tease my nipples, stroke my belly. She's gentle, now; mollifying against the goosebumps that have prickled across my flesh. Anticipation of her bite rises in me, threatening to spill over, but she glides her hands soothingly across my skin as she whispers, "Hush, easy my love, don't you worry . . ." into the crook of my neck. A calm sweeps over me. The eye of our storm.

It's so slow and so smooth, almost tender, that it takes a moment for me to be sure I'm not imagining it: the stinging puncture of her fangs. I wonder, hazily, if she's always had fangs? Have I ever seen them? My eyes jag blearily to the mirror before I remember, with half a laugh, that she's not there. Two small, fascinating holes gape in the curve of my neck, growing as she fills me, and I can't look—I just feel the pressure, fullness, her mouth one with my flesh. She's moaning, low and resonant. But then all I can hear is my pulse slamming in my ears and I wonder absently if she can hear it too—if it's hers too, what I'm hearing. I'm full, so full—

and I realize, clenching, that her fingers have speared into my pussy as well, and time has stopped and I'm not sure how we're still upright as she's inside me, filling me—everywhere.

And then, too soon but also—*yes, finally*, she's slipping out of me, lapping fervently at my wound with her tongue like it's the best thing she's ever tasted, holding my throat firmly with one hand. She is also rubbing my clit with slick fingers, making the same broad sweeps as her tongue on my neck and I search, straining and trembling against her hands and face, for the ache, for searing pain . . . but I can't find it. I'm lost in pleasure, swimming, drowning—and I want more, need it to sting.

Then I feel her lips close around my wound, and it's sharp and sudden when she begins to draw from me.

I cry out in relief as my veins burn, throbbing under the pull of her, the suction. I'm grinding my clit against her palm, arched so I'm pressing my neck against her lips and harder, into the sharp edge of her teeth. Lilith isn't sipping: she drinks me desperately, sucking, and I wonder if I hope she knows her limits—my limits. In this moment, I'm not sure I'd want her to stop if she reached them. I think—I want her to consume me whole.

All at once, I notice that I'm light as a feather. Am I dreaming? Is this real? I force my eyes partway open to look in the mirror, and blearily register from the angled view that my head is lolling, my body . . . levitating? Closing my eyes again, I use my last shreds of thought to piece together that between her firm grip around my middle, and her fingers fucking deep and hard inside me, she is holding my full weight, suspending me, possessing me. I'm not sure I'm human anymore, not sure I belong on planet Earth because I might float up, might already be on clouds, among the stars bursting behind my eyelids as I'm being born, or dying, or maybe coming, convulsing within the solid grip of her arms.

When my eyes open again, Lilith is hovering over me, smirking.

"There you are," she croons. "I knew you'd come around. How do you feel, darling?"

I register, dimly, the dark sheets of her bed, her silk pillowcase under my cheek, musky scented candles flickering on the nightstand. My head still feels light—my whole body, really—like I might be floating an inch off the mattress. I feel my pulse thrumming faintly in my fingertips, my toes, my tongue, my clit . . . and each beat tickles, a little flutter of satisfaction. It might be the candles, but I'm pretty sure I'm actually glowing. Lilith is too, for sure. She's luminous in the dim room, beaming down at me like the moon.

"I feel . . . incredible."

"As you should, my love. You *are* incredible."

"Can I—" I'm trying to remember one of my fleeting thoughts as I struggle to recall the moments and sensations from earlier. "Can I see your teeth?"

Lilith laughs, delighted. "Of course!" She smiles brightly, and it's just—my Lilith, beautiful and sweet. There's nothing remarkable about her grin, besides an adorable hint of an overbite and the dimple that creases her freckled cheek.

"Then . . . then how . . ."

"We'll skip the mirror next time, shall we? I didn't want to scare you, face to face, your first time. But if you're into it, if—if you want to stick around—"

"Oh, *definitely*," I interrupt.

I think, then, that she . . . blushes? It's not a look I've seen on her before, and I wonder with a flutter if it's *my* blood in her cheeks. "I'm so glad," she murmurs quietly, and leans down for a kiss, whispering against my lips, "You are *delicious*."

TEN

Yarn & Yearning

by Mary Helen Gallucci

Part 1

Sophia

I'm at Juniper's Art Supplies, perusing their buy-one-get-one bead sale, when I hear her. It's some girl right on the other side of the display I've been inspecting, which I can tell from her conversation is the yarn aisle. I have to pretend an interest in the details of an amber crackle strand so I can lean a little closer to hear her through the deep padding of the yarn.

"—Just *one last* skein of my super-soft Caron Big Cakes Peach Part-ay yarn to finish off my lesbian flag blanket tomorrow at—" she's saying, her voice rising in frustration. I don't hear any response before she adds, "—No, I found it, I just can't fucking *reach* it . . . hang on." Something clatters, and I'm guessing it's her phone she's setting down before the muffled thud of her feet landing hard on the floor. She huffs a windy exhale before emitting the most adorable *"hyup"* I've ever heard, followed quickly by another heavy thud. "I gotta go," she says. "Gotta find a stool or an employee or something. Yeah, talk to you later."

There's a little frustrated groan, and then one more *"hyuuuh"* followed by a clash and clatter. "Oww, fuuuuck meeee," she gripes so quietly I can barely make it out. I'm stifling a laugh while also feeling startlingly endeared to the disembodied voice of this apparently short, apparently clumsy, apparently crafty and gay girl in the next aisle over. As her footsteps retreat, I hope she's looking for that stool or employee, not giving up . . . and I find myself hastening around the corner to catch a glimpse of her, my curiosity way too piqued to let her vanish a mystery.

We very nearly collide at the endcap of the aisles, and as she bounces back from me she lets out a startled "OH!!"–her phone clattering out of her coat pocket onto the floor.

She scrambles to grab it, and without thinking, I'm asking, "Hey, can I help you?"

She straightens. Squints at me skeptically. "You work here?"

"N-no," I stammer. I'm realizing I don't actually want to admit to eavesdropping, so I add, "I just meant—you dropped your phone, I thought I—I could—"

She quirks an eyebrow so distinctly, I'm momentarily mesmerized by her face. Her features are all so pronounced, that quizzical expression so effortless, I think absently for a moment that she should be in commercials, or *movies*, or—

"You thought you could . . . pick . . . it up?" she finishes for me, brandishing the no-longer-floor-bound phone in her open palm.

"Yeaaah," I mutter sheepishly. "Never mind, sorry."

"Oh my god," she laughs. "You're *adorable,* you're all pink! Listen, I'd say you actually *could* help, but you actually might be shorter than I am . . . What are you, five-foot-even?"

"I'm five-one," I manage.

"Oh," she says, "me too. You just seem kinda tiny, no offense. I actually bet I could lift you, if you wanna try it?"

I feel my eyes bug out at her for a moment before she hastily adds, "WAIT, I meant like—so we could reach! The top shelf, my yarn . . . Jesus, I'm sorry, that was so weird and you literally have no idea what I'm talking about . . ."

Now *she's* flushing, but also I'm noticing the thickness of her forearms and the edge of a tattoo extending from the rolled cuffs of her flannel. I babble, "Oh—yeah no, sure, let's do it, I'm in!"

"Really?!" she says, her eyes lighting up. "Oh my god, thank you! I promise I won't make it weird—or, *weirder* . . ." She shoves her phone back into her pocket and then grabs my arm, pulling me back down the aisle she'd emerged from.

"Okay," she says, stopping us abruptly in the middle of the yarn display that must soar at least seven feet up there. The "shelves" are not so much shelves as a system of wire baskets, with a lip preventing the stacks of yarn from tumbling down in an avalanche. She points, then jumps, jabbing up at a large ball of peach-pink gradient. "That's the one we're after. I ordered a bunch of it online but it took, like, three weeks to arrive, and I *thought* I had enough but one of the skeins just— disappeared? It must be in a box in my house *somewhere,* unless I actually used them all up and just . . . didn't notice? I don't understand? Anyway, sorry, I just need one more of that exact one, in time for book club tomorrow or I won't have anything to crochet and it'll be *awkward.*"

I blink. "Why do you need yarn for book club?"

"Oh I host this . . . we call it 'Yarn and Yearning': we

discuss a queer book every month while knitting or crocheting or something. Keeps all our ADHD hands busy and we don't have to make eye contact or like, try to be clever or anything? It's just chill, it's nice."

She looks me up and down and I'm shot through with a pang of hope that she's about to invite me, because that sounds . . . incredible? Who is *we?* But instead she just says, "Okay if you're cool with it, can I just—come stand right here." She shrugs off her bright dandelion-yellow coat, tossing it in onto a nearby shelf. Then she steps back and points to the spot on the floor where she'd been standing. Dutifully, I take her place, and then her arms are around my waist and she's flush against my back going "HYUP" all over again. My feet leave the ground, but like—*barely*, and I'm immediately laughing so hard I forget to even try to reach for the yarn. She drops me back down (a whole three inches), laughing wildly herself.

"I'm sorry, I'm sorry!" I gasp for air, "I don't think that's gonna work that way, though!"

"You didn't even *try!!*" she shrieks, grabbing me again. "Actually *reach* this time!!"

I do, stretching my arms overhead as she heaves me up, but the best I can do is poke the yarn through the wires with my fingertip. She drops me again, still laughing, and then covers her face with her hands. "I can't believe I'm saying this but can you like . . ." She holds her palm out and undulates her middle fingers, curling them toward her palm and then straightening them again. It's fluid, like a *very* practiced motion. My face is hot and I can't look away. "—Like, urge it forward through the slats?"

"Do you want me to just lift you?" I ask, but she's shaking her head before I even finish.

"No way, I'm like twice your size. Look, what if I . . ." She gets down on one knee and I'm blushing *even more, god damnit.* A crazy image flashes before my eyes of finding some skin tone in the paint section and slathering it all over my flaming face with a foam brush. Or maybe just face-planting into a tray of it, or like—a clown getting pied at the carnival . . .

But she's *looking* at me, and *smirking,* some kind of analysis going on behind her eyes. "Here, hold my hand for balance and I'm your stool. Then do the finger thing like I showed you," she instructs, patting her thigh and grabbing my hand. Mine is a little sweaty but hers feels strong and a little rough— in a good, utilitarian way. I totally trust her, I think.

Giggling nervously, I hesitate, then toe my shoes off before climbing onto her. I'm immediately unsteady, my socked feet wrapping around her thigh and toes squeezing hopelessly as I shake off her hand and grasp the baskets with both of mine. "WHOA," she warns, as the baskets shift against each other with a clang. "Oh my god look out!"

The whole row shifts again; something has come unhooked, and then another invisible something springs free back there and it's all tipping toward me when I let go and jump down. A skein bounces down and rolls across the floor, followed by the one behind it, and the one behind that . . . There's an avalanche of yarn bouncing off my head, and this isn't even the right row of them, dammit! We needed the row on top.

"So, not a gymnast, are we?" she observes dryly.

"I'm so sorry . . ." I begin, but she's laughing as she scurries to collect the fallen merchandise, tossing it back into the now-off-kilter baskets.

"It's all good! They aren't *my* baskets! You'd think they'd be sturdier . . ." Then she chews her lip. It's really a very full, lovely pink lip, I notice. "Well, there's only one thing left to try," she says.

I nod, resigned. Time, I suppose, to give up and go find an employee. I feel bad for having been useless, and extra *extra* embarrassed that I'll have to explain their busted basket system, but I'll take one for the team. She needs that yarn, after all.

"Guess you need to get on my shoulders."

I choke. "W-what?!" I sputter.

"I'll get down, you climb on, and I'll stand up. I do squats every day, I got this."

"Ohhhh no no no," I say, still feeling the vertigo of my most recent mishap in my belly. And possibly some other kind of vertigo as well.

"I got you! I'll hold your legs. We'll be bottom-heavy, it'll be fine. You'll be plenty high enough, no finger trick needed. Lift—grab—done."

"On your . . . shoulders?" I repeat, so *so* aware I sound dumb as bricks; but I *might be*, because I can't even picture what she's describing. "Won't I like, pop your head off?"

"Oh my god." She's laughing so hard at me and I can't help but laugh too. I might be a little giddy. She might be too, the way she's clutching her chest. "Don't you have any kids in your life?!"

"I mean, I have a nephew, but—"

"Please," she gasps, "don't be offended, but you must be the most boring aunt ever?! How is this a crazy idea to you?"

"First of all I was gonna say he's nineteen—" She claps a hand on my shoulder, leaning heavily as she doubles over. "And how is this *not* a crazy idea? In any world?!"

"We need to *broaden your horizons,* baby," she tells me, kneeling low and bracing her hands on the floor to, presumably, hold my weight. "Starting right now, let's go-o-o!"

"You will one hundred percent drop me, you're like already shaking!" I protest. But I also can't just leave her hanging like that, on the floor as she is, so I step up behind her and place my hands gingerly on her back like we're two grown women playing leap frog right here in the middle of the craft store.

"Nonono," she says. "Come in front and sit, like you're gonna sit on my . . . head, just don't actually."

"You're telling me to sit on your . . . head," I echo.

"I'm telling you *not* to, you dolt!" Then she interrupts her own laughter to ask me abruptly, "Sorry, are you gay?"

"*What?*" It feels like I'm dreaming at this point. Who asks questions like this? "Am I . . . Ah . . . a little?"

She plops on her ass. "A *little?!*" she shrieks. "What does *that* mean?"

"It—it means yes, ok? I was thrown by the weird question! Are *you?*"

That's when a Juniper's sales associate clears his throat and says "Uhh . . . can I help you ladies?"

I don't even realize how raucously loud our giggles have been till they stop. Now the silence feels deafening as we come to, looking sheepishly at each other's shiny red faces and the absolute mess of yarn and shelving baskets surrounding us.

"Fuck," she murmurs (what even is her name?), and then says cheerfully, "Oh my god *yes*, thank you, can you just grab something for me quick? We couldn't reach."

He retrieves the correct ball like it's nothing—the guy's gotta be six-foot-two—then starts re-hooking the baskets. They're still bent a little off-kilter but he graciously doesn't mention it. "Anything else I can help you with?" he offers. When we decline he adds, "Have a nice day!" We look from him to our mess, and I'm stooping to begin picking it up when he finishes, "Thank you for shopping at Juniper's!" so pointedly, we take the hint and scurry away.

Once we round the corner toward the cash registers, we

both erupt again. I'm just trying to collect my wits and breath to ask her name when she wheezes, "Of *course* I am, were you kidding?"

"You are—what?"

"I'm *obviously* gay, I mean . . ." She gestures to the blue streaks in her hair with a good-natured roll of her eyes as we settle into the self-checkout line, then pulls up the cuff of her flannel to reveal a forearm tattoo of a frog sitting on a rainbow-speckled mushroom. "Besides, I literally told you I'm making a lesbian flag blanket and host a sapphic book club . . . do you hear anything I say?!"

She's leaned in to try to make eye contact, which I realize when my gaze finally releases the tattoo on her forearm. "Wow," I breathe; then, "Yes, *yes*, I swear I'm listening, stuff just . . . takes me a minute when I'm . . ."

I trail off and she smirks. "When you're what?"

"Um . . . stunned," I admit.

"Oh, I'll take that! Hey, do you wanna come?"

"Come where?"

She scans her item as she rattles off: "Sapphic book club, silly goose. Yarn and Yearning. You wanna come? It's okay that you didn't read the book, plenty of people don't. But you knit, right? Or crochet? You were in the yarn aisle . . . oh god, did you get what you needed? We can go back for it, grab something from the costuming aisle for a disguise . . ."

"Y-yeah! I mean—no," I stammer, not sure where to begin with the barrage of questions. "I didn't really need anything, and I think that guy super wanted us out of here ASAP—"

"Okay! Here—" she snatches the receipt as the machine spits it out, then produces a tiny mini pen from the carabiner full of keys and gadgets she'd had stuffed into her pants pocket. "Six—three—six—four—Ollllive Rooooad," she narrates, scribbling on the back of the receipt. "And—here's my number, text me if you have any questions or anything! Or . . . I mean yeah, y'know: anything!"

She's skipped bagging; just hands me the receipt, re-pockets her pen and carabiner, and shrugs back into her coat, stuffing the yarn into one side of it and then tying the belt at her waist in a secure knot. She looks like the world's worst shoplifter and I just can't believe my eyes. It's ridiculous and also somehow the most endearing thing I've ever seen.

"Wait," I say, halting as she marches toward the exit. I have so many questions, I'm not sure where to begin. But I do have her number now, so I guess I could just text her? Still, something feels unfinished, and I'm reluctant to let her walk right out the door.

Both sets of automatic double doors hiss open, waiting, as I gape at her, trying to decide what to ask. A gust of wind picks up and snowflakes billow in. A child at the next checkout counter whines about the cold. "Just come on?!" this absurd adorable mystery girl urges me. "Your car's out here some-where too, right? You drove?"

When I step forward, she takes my arm in hers, huddling close against the wind to share body heat like we've been best friends forever. Best—queer—friends forever. "Friends." Who almost sit on each other's heads. But also don't know each other's names.

"Where'd you park?" she asks me.

"Of all the unimportant questions," I laugh through gritted teeth.

But she yells, "*WHAT?*" into the wind, and I realize it's actually extremely relevant. I shuffle her to my car, parked blessedly close, and when I open the driver's side door, she immediately hops in ahead of me, scooching over to the passenger side. I am, once again, stunned at her audacity. "Well get in, get in!" she urges me. "I'm not kidnapping you, it's *your* car, Jesus! Start the engine, it's fucking freezing!!"

"Do you . . . need a ride?" I ask as I follow her instructions.

"No no, I'm just on the other side of the lot, but it seemed like you had something to say and we needed to get out of that store since they hate us now."

I sit on my hands as the car begins to blast cold air through the vents. "Oh—yeah. Um, what book is the discussion about tomorrow?"

"Right! It's *Kiss Her Once for Me*—you know, that Alison Cochrun holiday book that came out a couple years ago?"

"Oh hey, yeah! I actually listened to that like, right away—preordered it and everything, it was so good!" I find myself bouncing a little and I'm not sure if it's the cold or the sheer thrill of hearing this girl speaking my language. She's got a prefab group of queer girls I already fit right in with? It's absolutely too good to be true—and yeah, it kind of isn't completely true, but I push this from my mind to worry about at a later date, as she's talking again and I need all my focus to redirect my attention from the fireworks exploding in my body.

"No way! You're all set! It's like we were meant to run into each other! I've been just *dying* to discuss how steamy that snowed-in only-one-bed scene was—and the firewood chopping?!"

"*PLEASE*," I groan. "Honestly I might have to listen to those couple chapters again tonight—you know, as a refresher."

"You have it on you?"

"Oh, I guess, yeah—it's in my app on my phone . . ."

"You wanna put it on now? I read it looky-booky style, now I wanna hear it!"

I fish my phone from my pocket and start scrolling with a stiff thumb. "Oh my god that's such a great—" All of a sudden I stop in my tracks, and look over at her. She's grinning at me with bright eyes, her lower lip between her teeth, cheeks rosy. She looks like art, like the universe placed a color-pop filter on just her in the dark drab winter night, her skin and dandelion jacket glowing somehow in the muted light of my dashboard. And she wants to just . . . casually listen to a sex scene together in my car? Like that's a normal studious book club brush-up? A study group of two?

"Y-yeah," I conclude, "let's do it!" My thumb is jittery and I keep hitting the wrong thing, but if this girl wants to stay in my car and walk this line of—what is it really, flirting? Unclear, but I'm *so* in.

I finally get the book called up and make an educated guess at what chapter begins the snowed-in section. It takes a few stabs, and then—there they are, in the blizzard, finding the cabin. I skip forward a bit more, then set my phone in its dash cradle as the narration fills the car, pulling my legs up to cross them under me and get comfy. The air is finally coming in hot, and I look up to see she's untied her yellow coat, and is fingering the citrusy lesbian yarn in her lap. Her flannel is unbuttoned enough that she's got *cleavage* and it's like looking into the sun. My blush heats me to my toes. I shrug out of my coat, too.

I'm not sure if I'm more lost in the heat of the story or the electricity of this cabin of my car, but before I can really come to my senses, the girls in the book are kissing against a wall and the girl sitting next to me is reaching across the console to tangle her fingers in mine. Then I realize she's tugging a little, wordlessly so as not to interrupt, and when I look up at her face, her expressive eyes are so wide and hopeful and her cheeks are so pink and her lips are so wet, I can't miss her meaning. She smiles broadly as I crawl over the gear shift, and it somehow doesn't feel awkward at all, facing her in her lap. I guess we got physical barriers out of the way back in the store, because being in her arms is familiar already.

The only difference is, now we're not giggling. She looks so earnest right now—so different from the blustery forward goofball I'd pegged her as, and the range has me a little bit in awe. She's *beautiful,* my god. I pass my thumb over her flushed cheek, and her long lashes flutter closed. We're breathing each other's breath. I'm melting into her arms, sinking, our bodies fitting and forming together perfectly until my lips—finally—find hers. They're slow and so soft. I slip my fingertips gently into her hair and it's silk, and somehow incredibly intimate, and she whimpers just a little. So briefly my ears immediately feel the loss of it, regretting the speakers' audio that's slipped so far to the back of my mind. I'm *thirsty* for more sounds from her—and then my memory calls up her absolutely endearing little *hyuh* noises from back in the store, and I've never wanted someone so badly in my life.

I take her lower lip in my teeth. Her hand is pressing my lower back, sneaking just a touch under my sweater, and I'm hyper-aware of the contact point with her skin—and of where my open thighs squeeze against her torso—as the tip of my tongue dips to brush her lip, almost reverently. She whimpers again and it's *delicious,* tugging at my heart and melting lower. I *want* her. Her chest presses against mine, rising and falling unsteadily as she gasps against our kiss, then returns with even more eagerness. I'm emboldened, sliding my palm from her cheek, to her throat, and down between us to cup her breast—

That's when my car sputters off.

Part 2

Brandi

"Oh, FUCK no."

She's still in my lap, twisting and pawing at her car's dials to stop the audiobook. When the narrator's voice cuts out, there's dead silence.

My magical yarn girl stares down at me with wide eyes. "What's going on?"

"I super needed to stop for gas on the way home," she confesses breathlessly. "I kind of got . . . distracted . . . and forgot."

"Oh my god, it's my fault!!" I exclaim, mortified. "I distracted you!!"

"No!" she insists hastily, before adding, "I mean, obviously yes, but it's my stupid fault for running it on empty. My dad used to always tell me to stop that and I never listened. . . . I mean, to be fair, this is the first time it's actually bitten me in the butt. I did know I was risking it, I just . . . y'know, didn't count on a . . . all this." She's gesturing vaguely at me, looking so anxious, and I think I actually feel her trembling a little in my arms.

"Yeah, hey it works out though," I tell her, in as soothing a tone as I can manage. "I'm here now, we can take my car to a gas station and figure it out."

She shudders against the cold air that's begun pouring through the vents now that the engine is off, and I grab her coat from the driver's seat to wrap around her shoulders, then pull her closer into a hug. Outside, the lamp post we're parked next to highlights giant white clusters falling wetly and accumulating in the dark, emptied-out parking lot. Then I notice that her reflection in the window is blinking back tears.

"Hey—hey!" I kiss her head, and it feels oddly intimate but also just right? She melts into me a little, and our eyes lock in the window's reflection. "Or, I can just drive you home and we can deal with it tomorrow?"

"We? Tomorrow?" she asks, voice small. "You'd do that? I could just . . . call an uber in the morning or something . . ."

"Hey, I got us into this mess, I'm not ditching you to some uber driver. Plus like, what if she's cuter than me?" I grin at her in the window, and oh my god from that wobbly smile I can tell she's trying so hard to keep it together and it's *extra* endearing right now. She laughs a little despite herself, then sits up a little to kiss me. My chest floods with so much warmth I don't even miss the car's heat.

"Literally impossible," she murmurs, settling her weight against my chest.

I hug her tight. "So."

"So," she echoes.

"What is your name, mystery yarn girl?"

She laughs again, and her in giddy stitches in my arms feels like relief and like maybe we're already home, out here in the dead car. "I literally thought you'd *never* ask. It's Sophia."

"MmmmMMMmm! Hey Sophia," I purr, playfully lowering my voice a couple steps, "I'm Brandi. Can I take you home?"

"Does that mean we have to move?" she asks against my shoulder. "I dunno how this is so comfy . . ."

"We could just . . . move this to someplace where we won't potentially die of exposure?"

Sophia snorts a little. "So that's my third option?"

"Yep—if we don't wanna go get gas in this snow-pocolypse, and you don't wanna have to call me in the morning, sounds like I'm keeping you tonight. If—that sounds best to you? I mean"—I add, suddenly aware of how forward I'm being to this poor stranded girl I just met five minutes ago and already kissed—"no pressure, that just seems like a clear solution to this conundrum."

"Mm-hm," she agrees. "Makes sense. Let's go." She continues to sit on me, motionless.

"Okay, cool." I shift my hips a little. "Hey so I know I kept telling you I'm crazy buff and all, but like, this angle was not what I had in mind when I said I could lift you easy."

She cracks up again, and damn if I don't feel like a million bucks every time I hear that. I nuzzle in to kiss her vibrating neck.

"C'mon Brandi, it's your time to shine!" she giggles, tipping her head back to give me access. "This car isn't getting any warmer!"

"Actually," I say between tiny kisses, "I think we could heat it up a little if we really wanted to . . ."

Sophia shudders again, but this time I'm certain it's not a chill. "Fuck," she whispers softly.

Then she shakes her head like she's clearing an etch-a-sketch. I sit back. "How far away do you live?" she asks, her voice rough.

"Just, like, five minutes," I tell her. "Maybe ten with the roads like this. You really sure you wanna come over?"

"Yeah, if that's okay, I really do."

"More than okay," I assure her.

She lets out a long breath. "Okay, for real this time," she says. Then she takes my face in her slim icy fingers and kisses me, deliberately. "Thank you. So much."

That's not what I was expecting. "Hey, believe me, I'm beyond happy to be here right now."

She grabs my yarn from the driver's seat and presses it snugly against my currently way-too-sensitive breast, before pushing her arms into her jacket and zipping it up. Then she's climbing off me, and I immediately miss her. As soon as I tie the sash on my own coat, the car door opens and we're tumbling over each other out into the snow.

"Welcome to my home," I announce, pulling the back door shut behind us as we stomp the snow off our shoes onto my rainbow doormat.

"Wow," she breathes, looking around with wide eyes. I watch her face as she takes in my kitchen: the patterned wallpaper, my tiled backsplash, my blue cabinets, the yellow accents. I instantly regret that there's clutter on the counter and table, and the dishwasher is yawning open; but it's not like I'd planned to impress a girl tonight.

"Yeaaah, it's kind of a mess, sorry," I say, cringing. "I'd meant to tidy up before Yarn & Yearning folks show up tomorrow. At least the floor was recently mopped?"

Sophia shakes her head. "It's *beautiful.*" She toes off her shoes and begins wandering around to look at the little details. The faces on the gourd-shaped ceramic ingredient canisters on the counter, the depth of my yellow porcelain farmhouse sink, the knobs and switches on my nostalgia coffee machine. "Is the whole house like this?"

"Pretty much, yeah. I moved in last year, it's been kind of

my . . . other . . . crafty hobby, y'know. I DIY-remodel all the little things I can."

"I bet these windows over the sink are *gorgeous* in daylight," she says. "What direction are they facing?"

"East," I tell her. "I saw this trick online where if you paint the insides of the panes yellow like that, it looks like . . . *extra* sunny all the time."

"I *love* it," she says emphatically. "Like, it's the middle of the night and it *does*, it's like we stepped out of midwest winter and into a different time zone or something." Then she gasps, "Ooh! I have the *perfect* beads to hang in them. They'd look incredible with your . . ."—she waves a hand vaguely—"decor scheme. They'll throw rainbows everywhere in the direct morning light!"

That is possibly the best idea I've ever heard—and I've spent a lot of time brainstorming in this very kitchen. And it was just—up her sleeve? I'm *thrilled*. "Oh my god, I need them. And also? I *need* to kiss you, if that's okay with you."

Her attention snaps suddenly to me, and her smile brightens her whole face. "*Please*," she says earnestly, wrapping her arms around me. And then, "Can you show me your bedroom?"

"Absolutely." I kiss her once—twice—and then take her hand, trying not to tug it with urgency. "This way."

When we get to my room, there's a heap of blankets and knitted squares covering my bed, and I hastily shove them to the wall to make room for two. "I know I'm like a walking stereotype—look, I don't have other people in here often . . ."

"You've made *all* these?!" She's fingering an especially soft square that had been on the floor. It has a little daisy in the middle, and she threads her fingertips delicately between the woven petals.

"Yeah," I say a little sheepishly. "It's not that I have tons of downtime, exactly, It's just nice to multitask, and I love the feel of it on my hands while I'm using my brain for other things, you know?"

Something—I'm not sure if it's skepticism or confusion, maybe?—flashes across her face for a second, and then she puts down the square and climbs on the bed. "This is *the* coziest place I've ever been. You'll hate my apartment. I kind of do too, now."

She pulls one of my more complete blankets from the pile —a rainbow block one—and drapes it over herself, snuggling into it like a giant gay cocoon. Then she looks up and holds it open to me as an invitation. I waste no time joining her.

"You still haven't kissed me much," she whispers.

So I do. Her lips are so soft, and warm, and sweet, and I feel her smile against mine. She's rubbing the length of her body against mine just a little, like she still needs some friction to finish thawing, or maybe just needs to be closer. I catch her bottom lip and taste it, the tip of my tongue running along it and she moans deliciously. Her hand has found my breast again, through my sweater, like it had in the car right before everything sputtered to a halt. She seems like, *really* interested in my chest, maybe kind of despite herself? And I feel my nipples pricking almost painfully in their eagerness for that attention from her.

"Can I take off my shirt?" I ask, and my voice comes out so breathless I barely recognize it.

"*Yes,*" she says, catching my eye for a charged moment before I'm sitting up to pull it off and she's watching, captivated. I'm just wearing an old stretched-out sports bra underneath, and honestly if she's gonna be seeing some of my curves I'd just as soon have her see all of them, so I pull that off too.

. . . A moment passes and I think she's holding her breath?

I'm so aware of my peaked nipples now, it's like she's touching them with her eyes—but an actual touch would be such a relief at this point . . .

"Fffffuck . . . me," she finally whispers on the exhale. I'm grinning—I can't help it. She's chewing her lip so fucking cute when I take her limp hand and place it over my breast. "Guu-uuhhhh," she groans. And wow it's so flattering, like her whole face is bright pink and I've never seen pupils so wide. I forget what color her eyes even were, because now they are all a steamed-up black. I wouldn't just *assume* someone was crazy into me, but there's literally no other way to take this girl, and I'm kind of obsessed.

Then she rubs her thumb over my nipple and it's my turn to groan. She pinches and pulls, experimentally, and I'm already *way* too close to exploding, just from the focus and tension and satisfaction of the last two minutes. I lean down over her, hovering, offering my breast to her mouth. She takes it so eagerly, I huff a laugh. She's so fucking beautiful, and I tell her so. She just hums in response, apparently too committed to free her mouth for speech right now.

Her tongue tastes me and sucks me; I feel my nipple passing over and under it, now gently between her teeth, now deep to the back of her throat, her jaw opening wide to take more of my flesh. She gags a moment and I'm about to apolo-gize when she shakes her head vehemently, sucking with such enthusiasm that I think I might come from the sight and feel and just the fucking *vibes* of this girl fucking my breast with her mouth like she's spent her life starving for it.

I shift to press her thigh between my legs, and she releases me for only one bare needy moment before locking onto my other nipple, and then I'm coming in earnest. I wasn't ready and it hits me like a steam engine, fast and so hard. I jerk too far, uncontrollably; there's a pop as I'm ripped from her suction, and I hear myself shriek at the loss. I'm grinding on her leg and she's pushing back so good, drawing me out until she's palming both breasts and *squeezing*.

I don't know what all noises I've been making, but when my eyes finally open and I wager a glance at her face, she's flushed and panting like *she* just had the screaming orgasm way sooner than intended, not me. She's looking at me like I'm some sort of goddess, holding my breasts like chalices, and by all things holy I am going to fuck her *so good*.

"You are . . . incredible," she tells me breathlessly.

"Okay take off your clothes," I demand. "Please. I mean, if you want to, but like. Really I hope you're ready because I'm dying to take you right now."

Her eyes widen and I realize I've maybe come on a little strong despite my best intentions. I'm trying to leave her an out because I know I just met her, and it's possible I could read her wrong . . . but she *seems* for all the world like an open book with her heart on her sleeve—or something like that that makes more sense, but sue me, I can't think straight right now. "Anyway like no pressure but I'm absolutely happy for you to . . . you know, come sit on my face?"

"Not your head?" she says with a giggle.

"My head?" She's not making any moves to follow any of my suggestions and now I'm wondering what the fuck she's laughing about, but I'm lightheaded and a bit giddy and I can't help but laugh with her.

"At the store . . . you were lifting me and then you told me to sit on your head—"

"I think I told you *not* to sit on my head? And then *you* said something about getting off—"

"I said I didn't want to *pop it off*, your head, like a little lego guy! Oh my god you were thinking—and then that dude showed up—" She's giggling like a fiend and it's adorable but

I realize that even though she's for sure super gung-ho when *I* lead, she might be a little more nervous than I'd been giving her credit for.

"Hey so maybe we don't need heads popping off right now," I offer, kissing her rosy cheek before combing my fingers through her bed-mussed hair. "We could try one of our safer moves, if you're interested?"

"Brandi," she says, sobering a little, "That finger trick of yours. You've gotta be kidding me. That was for sure a move."

"Depends on what you mean by a move," I tell her. "I mean, would it have gotten the yarn out? Yes. Was I *hitting on* you? . . . Okay also yes."

She grins at me, nose to nose on the pillow. I'm topless over here, but no big deal—every time she glances down her pupils blow out a bit all over again, and she seems so content and comfy in my bed right now, it feels like this is going just right.

She looks like she's thinking about something, wheels turning. Then she says, "Okay."

"Okay?"

"Let's try that one."

"I'm not sure it qualifies as one of our safer moves," I can't help but quip. "It resulted in a yarn avalanche."

"I'm okay with risking it if you are," she whispers, her voice hitching a little.

"Yeah," I whisper back, cupping her sweet soft cheek and kissing her. "We got this," I promise.

She kisses me back earnestly, venturing with the tip of her tongue to touch mine, then explore the edge of my teeth, the roof of my mouth. It's so gentle it tickles in this *amazing* way and I sort of squeal before she draws back. "No—I like it," I tell her quickly. "Do it again."

As she does, I slip my hand from her jaw down her throat

to her collarbone, just at her shirt's neckline, fingering its ridge before moving to cup her breast over the material. "This okay?" I ask her, and then she captures my lips again before murmuring "mm-hmm" into them.

I massage her there, enjoying the softness and the way her back arches into me a little, the way her breath hitches when I find her nipple through the layers. "Mm-hmmmm," she hums again.

Reluctantly leaving her breast, I continue tracing a path down over her torso, over her hip, to her thigh. She's so warm —hot, really, the closer I get to her center . . . just steaming, actually—and the material of her leggings offers no friction at all as I skim my hand over and around, down the outside of her thigh and then up the inside. She's widening her hips, spreading her knees a tiny bit further every time I draw up toward the middle, and when I finally fold my palm between her legs she gasps, releasing my lips.

I kiss my way down her jaw to her throat, and now she's panting in earnest, little needy whimpers escaping in starts and fits, and my god I'm *barely* touching her. "Can I—"

"*YES,*" she groans before I can finish my question. I grin against the skin of her neck, licking and nipping her there as a little tease before I dip my hand under her waistband. And fuck, absolutely *fuck me* because her curls inside are so soft and *so goddamn drenched,* I'm surprised for a moment that I hadn't felt it pooling through her pants. That steaminess, though— she smells so delicious now, just fragrant in bloom as my fingers slip effortlessly between curls and folds. "Yes," she whispers again, ragged, when I find her center and circle it; then, "Fuck yesssssss," when I slide both of those two fingers into her—my "move," as promised.

Thank fuck she's so vocal and so wet or I'd worry two might've been a mistake. She's holding me tightly inside, squeezing, and squeezing her eyes shut too, not breathing at all through her parted swollen lips. "Hey," I say softly, "I got you." Her eyes blink open for a moment, catching mine. I pull out and roll my fingertips over her clit, so hot and slick with her juices. Then she exhales heavily, and when I press inside again, it's softer like she's released a little. I curl my fingers, stroking her g-spot, and make a mental note to tell her later that it's squishy and ridged a *bit* like a bundle of yarn in a basket.

I'm sliding and stroking, pressing and rubbing, kissing away the tension in her beautiful face. She's grinding against my palm at her own pace as she whimpers, and I'm following the intensity of her writhing until she squeezes my fingers— my whole hand—tight between her thighs, gasping.

"Thank you," she breathes. "Wow I came."

"Oh my god—thank *you*," I say back, a little awestruck. She's still holding my hand there with her thighs, where it's warm and soft and perfect. "Babe. You're *gorgeous.*"

She looks skeptical. "*You* are. *Look* at you. Sorry I like . . ." —she gestures to herself—"stayed like this?"

"Hey, no, don't be sorry—" I rush to assure her, but she interrupts me.

"I have a confession."

"Yeah?"

"I hadn't actually been with a woman before."

Ohhhh. Things click into place in my brain while the pool of fondness that's been growing in my chest threatens to flood its gates. I can still feel her clit under my thumb and I'm overwhelmed with the privilege of it. "Yeah? Well you were perfect. You *are* perfect," I say, maybe even a little too emphatically. So I add, "That's maybe a lot to say to a girl I just met in the yarn aisle, but I'm pretty sure it's a hundred percent true."

She huffs a little regretful laugh. "Wellllll, that's another thing . . ."

She's cringing and pinking up again, and I have no clue where this is going . . . "Oh my god, what?!"

"I didn't need yarn earlier. I was there for the beads, and I heard you, and you sounded cute and I—" She takes a deep breath and her face falls as she admits wretchedly, "I can't really come to your book club."

"You can't?" I'm totally puzzled.

"I don't even knit!" she wails, burying her burning face in her hands.

And I wrap her up in my arms, laughing even as I hug her, because she's just the most adorable thing and I can't believe I was lucky enough that she wandered into my yarn chaos tonight. "No worries," I whisper into her ear, still smiling. "I can't wait to teach you."

ELEVEN

Love Me Tender

by Natalie Naudus and Mary Helen Gallucci

When I walk through the door, expecting the smells of dinner and the sound of music playing, I'm greeted with silence. Something is wrong.

"Helena? Babe?"

"I'm in here," she moans from the bedroom.

I drop my bag by the door and slip my shoes off, hurrying through the apartment. And there she is: my beautiful sad baby, curled around a pillow in the shape of an *S*.

"Baaaby!" I croon, immediately climbing into bed and wrapping myself around her. "What's the matter?"

"I just . . ." She sniffles. "I started my period, and it's got my fibro flared up, and my hands hurt too bad to cook dinner, and I promised you dumplings for your birthday . . ."

"Baby girl," I cut her off. "Hush, you just rest, I got you."

"But it's your *birthday*, and I really wanted to have the apartment all clean, and—"

"Shhhhh. Baby. You know what I want for my birthday? Like, really, truly?"

"What?" She looks back at me, tears caught in her lashes,

so precious and vulnerable that my heart goes all soft and squishy inside.

"I want to take care of my baby, and I want you to rest and not fight me about this."

"But *baby*—"

"Hey, is it my day or not? Don't I get to pick what I want?"

She pouts adorably, and snuggles deeper into her pillow. "Ok, I'll try not to fight you about it."

"That's my good girl. You rest and I'll get dinner sorted." As I turn to leave, she reaches out and grabs my arm.

"Kiss my face, please?"

"Of course, my love." I lean over her, gently kissing the soft curve of her cheek, relishing the texture of her skin against my lips.

"Why are you so sweet to me?" she whispers.

"Because I love you. Because you are my precious baby. I just want to take care of you."

She sighs contentedly and relaxes against me, wrapping her arms around my middle to keep me in place. I shift to snuggle closer, but her face contorts in a wince.

"I'm so sorry, baby! Where does it hurt?"

"Everywhere," she moans pathetically.

"My poor girl. Where am I starting?" I ask, my hands gently roaming across her back, hoping it's more a comforting gesture than a painful one. Some days every nerve ending is on fire for her, but right now she's not letting me go.

"Mmmmm," she mumbles into her pillow, shifting to her tummy. "My lower back? Period."

"Can I sit on you?"

"Yes *please.*"

I straddle her thighs, keeping some of my weight on my knees, just in case. Then I slide my palms against her skin, under the hem of her sweater, rucking it up. Her back is so smooth, so warm, I hum at the delicious sensation of holding her in my hands. I can't resist leaning down to plant kisses into the small of her back, my thumbs sinking into the dimples at her pelvic bones. God, I love this woman. I hope she can feel it, little currents through my fingertips, as I start to rub gentle circles there, then firmer. Deeper, until I'm following the muscles roped under the surface.

Helena groans a little from the pressure, or maybe the friction, so I reach over to the nightstand where our jar of coconut oil is still open from last night, taking a generous scoop with my fingers and then melting it between my hands. Now I can glide over her skin, which glows in the lamplight, rosy from my ministrations. My muscles are burning a bit, so I lean forward to press my body weight into the heels of my palms, rocking her hips from one to the other.

"Mmmm, that's so nice," Helena murmurs into her pillow.

"How about your shoulders, baby?" I ask after a moment, smoothing my palms up to knead between her shoulder blades with my thumbs.

"Unggh," she groans in encouragement. After rising to help her off with her sweater and sports bra, I gently brush her hair off her shoulders and neck, then settle back onto the soft seat of her ass and shift my attention upwards.

When my arms are spent, warm and aching so good—like I've poured some strength from them into the beautiful body of my precious girl—I lay myself on top of her. We have our own sort of relationship, I think—her body and I. I'm obsessed with it: its crooks and crannies, its textures and sensitivities. I feel at home with it, inside it. I can't imagine any vessel more perfect for this woman I love so deeply, can't imagine her any other way . . . But also, there's a place deep down where I'm almost angry with it for the pain it causes her. It's strange, admiring its beauty and strength, while also knowing it's what's betraying her, at least at this moment. Yet all I can do is love it, because it's her. And she is perfect to me: every moment, every inch. I rub my cheek into the smooth, vast expanse of her upper back, slightly sticky and smelling of coconut.

Helena sighs contentedly, the sound amplified under my ear. I wonder if she's drifting off. I need to get some food in her before hunger makes her flare worse.

With a few soft kisses across her shoulder blades—and then a few more to the back of her neck, because I can't resist—I steal away to the kitchen. She's already prepped the dumpling filling, but hasn't made the wrappers. I'm shit at making and rolling out the dumpling skins, so I improvise, tossing some oil in a pan and frying up a scoop of the filling, then adding some leftover rice from the fridge. I drizzle on soy sauce and sesame oil and some chili crisp, scoop steaming portions into two bowls, and carry them into the bedroom.

She sits up. I place a pillow in her lap, throw a towel over it, and nestle her bowl into it. She takes it with a hum of thanks and raises a steaming spoonful to her mouth.

"Mmmm, delicious!" she says, putting her spoon down and reaching out to rest her hand on my arm. "Thank you, my darling."

"I'm glad it's good. Hey, you made the meat!"

"Yeah, I guess I did." She smiles as she takes another bite. I dig into my portion, enjoying the warm comfort of a bowl full of food. We eat in contented quiet until I'm scraping the last grains of rice from the bottom of my bowl, taking hers, and stacking them on the nightstand. I hand her a glass of water and shake out two ibuprofen from the bottle into her hand, and she takes them obediently.

"Spoon me?" she asks, and I do: one arm in the crook of her neck, the other wrapped around her, holding her breast through her t-shirt. She moans lightly in frustration, and I remove my arm.

"What, baby? Did I hurt you?"

"No! No, put your hand back please." I reach around her and tenderly hold her breast, more gently this time. I feel her nipple pricking against my palm, and she arches her back a little, grinding her ass against me.

"Can I help you?" I laugh.

"Pleeease?" she whines. "I'm sorry, I know I shouldn't do anything with my hands right now, but I just . . . want you . . ."

"Baby." I lift myself, turn her gently onto her back, and kiss her. I smooth her hair back from her face, and kiss her forehead, her temples, along her cheeks. She tilts her chin up as I kiss along her jawline, giving me access to her neck.

I love this feeling of her unfurling beneath me, relaxing and blooming at my touch. She's so warm, so open, so *mine*, and I drink in the feel of her through my fingertips, my lips, inhaling the scent of her. I reach my hand below the blanket and pull aside her shorts, her panties and pad, finding her slick and warm. Easing between her lush folds I trace her clit, and she groans in my arms.

"Mmm, *yes*, baby." She's gazing into my eyes with such love, such confidence that it takes my breath away. "It's . . . so nice"—she shudders—"to feel *good*, you know?"

"Yes, my darling," I whisper against her forehead. "Yes, let me take care of you."

We lay like that for a while, her trembling slowing into a deep relaxation as I play with her: gentle circles, deep strokes. I hold her tenderly as she writhes slowly with the music of our love, her gaze on me so sure and steady, her gentle gasps nourishment to my very soul. When I slip a finger inside her, I enter her so easily, her wetness coating me. My fingers pulse with pleasure, drinking in the closeness, the absolute velvet of her, and she breathes deeply from my arms, reaching up to touch my face gently.

"Yes, baby," she murmurs, pulling my face down for a kiss. I slip my tongue between her lips, her mouth is so warm and inviting. She opens her mouth, inviting me in further, and I curve my tongue to rub the spot on the roof of her mouth that I know she likes. She starts coiling beneath me and I curl a finger inside her, massaging her sensitive soft ridges, attentive to each gasp and groan and squeeze of her walls.

Then I shift myself down to focus my attention lower, pausing to slide off her shorts and panties before renewing my efforts. Two fingers inside her, my other hand gently but steadily teasing her clit, I lay my head on her belly and drink her in. She strokes my head where it rests, then winds her fingers in my hair, gripping tightly as her pleasure builds. When her hips begin to thrust against me, fucking my fingers, I know she's close. I keep my rhythm steady, letting her draw it out at her own pace, until she cries out, shuddering around my fingers, clutching me to herself desperately.

As she relaxes, panting and smiling, I grab her dark shorts to wipe my hands.

"But what about you, baby?"

"Helena. My love. I enjoy you so much, you really have no idea."

"I feel so good." She sighs happily, kissing me.

"Now you go put on pants and pick out a movie while I change the sheets."

. . .

As I strip off the sheets, I hear her running the shower in the bathroom, and I smile. How can I love *everything* about this girl? Even the sound of her showering is precious to me. She's humming, and I'm delighted to know that I did that: I lifted her mood. I feel so lucky that I'm the one who gets to be here for her.

I do still want my birthday dumplings, though. Hopefully she'll feel up to making them later this week.

I put the coziest flannel sheets on the bed, and toss the dirty ones straight into the washer, starting the load. Then I'm back in the kitchen, popping some popcorn and making us a drink.

She pads into the kitchen and heads for the fridge.

"Whatcha looking for babe?" I ask.

"Oh just something . . . You go sit on the couch and I'll bring it to you."

"Baby, just let me—"

"No," she insists. "Let me do this for you! Go sit down!"

"Ok!" I laugh. "Yes, ma'am."

"And you pick out the movie, it's your birthday!"

I sit on the couch with the popcorn and start browsing, listening to Helena opening drawers and doing something in the kitchen. I wonder what she's got. I didn't see anything in the fridge, but maybe I missed it? I've just decided to watch an old comfort film when she comes out carrying a gorgeous lemon bar, a single glowing candle casting warm light on her face.

"Happy birthday, baby!"

"Helena, a lemon bar? From Corner Bakery? How did you hide it from me?!"

"I hid it in an empty Diet Dr. Pepper box!" She giggles. "I thought it would be safest."

"You sneaky hobbit."

"You pick your movie?" she asks, snuggling up next to me on the couch. I put the lemon bar on the table and blow out the candle, fanning away the wisps of smoke with my hand.

"Well, you said I could pick, but I kind of just want a *Lord of the Rings* rewatch. Is that ok?"

"Uuuuugh," she groans good-naturedly. "I suppose it's *fine*. It is your *birthday*, after all."

I laugh at her performative annoyance. I know she loves watching these as much as I do.

"Hey, Galadriel isn't going to lust after herself," I joke.

"Neither is *Legolas* . . ." She elbows me meaningfully.

"I've said it once and I'll say it again: he's the only man that has my attention."

"Babe, he's not even a *man*. He's an *elf*."

"Well, I guess I get to keep my lesbian card then!"

I hit play, and as Galadriel tells us what she feels in the water, the earth and the air, Helena snuggles deeper against me, tucking her feet under herself like the perfect cat she is. I kiss her softly on the forehead. She smells like home.

TWELVE

Roadside Assistance

by Natalie Naudus

"**A**re you fucking *kidding me?*" I kick at my tire and groan in frustration. Of course I have a flat. Of *course.* On the day that I have an international client in town for my most important meeting of the year. Balancing my coffee cup on top of my car, I dig in my purse for my phone, and call my roadside assistance service.

"We can have someone out to you in a mere three hours, ma'am," chirps the obnoxiously cheerful man on the other end of the line.

"Three hours?! What the hell am I paying you for?"

"We apologize for the inconvenience, but that's the earliest we can have someone to you! If you need someone sooner, we recommend dropping a line to your local auto shop or towing company! As I always say, if you need help fast, call triple Z last!"

"I . . . what? You *always* say that? Why is this the first I'm hearing about this? And why the hell is it so . . . you know what, it's not worth the energy."

"Would you like me to place-a-roo that work order for you, Ma'am? I'd be more than delighted to!"

I take a deep breath. Unclench my teeth. Wish I could unlatch my jaw like a snake and just devour this cheerful little agent entirely.

"Yes, that would be great. Thank you."

"My pleasure! We'll send a link to your phone so you can monitor their arrival time, or cancel if you no longer need their service. Have a sparkling day!"

"You too"—I hear him hang up—"you hyper-cheerful piece of shit my fucking god whyyyy?" I lean heavily against the side of my car, then pull away abruptly as I remember my suit. I'm vigorously brushing the dust off my pencil skirt when I hear a voice from somewhere nearby in the parking lot.

"You need some help?"

I look up and around, trying to locate the source. And then I see her: a tall, masc woman in coveralls, two parking spaces away. She's climbing out of a truck, one long leg planted firmly on the asphalt, her brown work boots worn and paint-splattered.

"Oh, I just . . . I have a flat tire." I explain, gesturing. "I've called roadside assistance, but they say it'll be a few hours."

"Well that's no good," she says, striding over and squatting down to take a closer look at my tire. She peers into the wheel well, and her fingers walk along the tire treads. Her nails are short and clean, her fingers strong and dusted with white paint. I find myself staring, and take a step away from her.

"Here's your problem: you've got a nail in your tire. A shop should be able to patch that for you pretty easily."

"Yes, well if you haven't noticed I'm not *at* a shop . . ." I stop as she turns and looks up at me, her eyes sparkling with amusement.

"No shit, Sherlock," she chuckles, casually looking me up

and down. "I gather from your fancy clothes that you have somewhere to be?"

"I . . . I'm sorry, I didn't mean to be rude. But yes, I have some important meetings today, and I'm pretty frustrated."

"You want me to throw the spare on for you?"

"The spare?"

"You do have a spare, don't you?"

"I . . . think so?" I'm blushing. "I'm sorry, I guess I should really know that, but this car is pretty new, and honestly cars are really not my thing.

"Pop your trunk and I'll take a look."

I obediently hit the clicker on my key fob.

"That's a good girl," she calls, and I find myself blushing furiously.

"Yeah, you've got a full-sized spare. Want me to throw it on for you? It'll get you to work, and you can take it to the shop tonight."

"Oh, if you don't mind . . ."

"Naw, it's no trouble; I'm just getting home from work. I work nights—renovations at the airport."

"Oh, I'd really, *really* appreciate it!"

I cancel the roadside assistance on my phone while she deftly jacks the car up and places the stands. In no time at all she has the wheel off, and is tightening the bolts on the spare.

"You like watching women work?" she asks laughingly. I realize I've been staring.

"Oh, I'm sorry. I mean, I like watching *you* work. I mean . . . you obviously know what you are doing with this . . . car . . . god I'm so sorry, thank you so much, please don't take . . . anything I'm saying seriously; I am such a mess . . ."

"Oh, please watch away," she interrupts me. "I like feeling your eyes on me."

Oh. My. God. Is she *flirting* with me? Wait, this *would* be an incredible meet cute. If I was brave enough to make a move . . .

"Do you want my number?"

"Excuse me?"

"God, I'm *so* sorry if I'm misreading things I just . . . you are very, very competent and attractive, and I thought maybe we could . . . But if I'm off base I'll just say thank you and . . ."

"No," she interrupts again.

"No?"

"No, but I'll give you mine." She hands me a card with a wink, and stands, wiping her hands off on her worn jeans. "I'll pack everything back in your trunk for you, then you are good to go!"

In a daze, I climb into my car, and hear her slam the trunk. Then she's back, propping her elbows on my open window, leaning into my space.

"You're all set."

"I don't know how to thank you, you've just . . . you are a *life* saver."

"I'd take a date, if you don't mind. Something tells me we'd get along . . . *really* well."

"I . . ." Warmth is pooling between my thighs at her closeness. Wisps of brown hair frame her face, and freckles are scattered across her cheeks.

"Can I bring you lunch tomorrow?" she asks me.

"Tomorrow? Oh, I . . . I work downtown in Victory tower."

"What floor?"

"Fortieth," I whisper. Why am I whispering? "Offices of McNeeland and Clark."

"I'll see you tomorrow . . ." She pauses, and I realize with a fluster that she's waiting for my name.

"Andi," I supply.

"I'll see you tomorrow, Andi. And if you want, feel free to wear that pencil skirt."

Only when she's gone do I look at her card in my hand. It says Lu Flagstaff, Flagstaff Renovations.

The next day, Lu pushes into my office in her coveralls, a brown paper bag in her hands.

"Lunch time?" She grins crookedly at me, and I stand from behind my desk, shuffling papers to the side and closing my laptop. I drink in the sight of her: short-cropped hair, asteroid-mining-astronaut sexy in her work clothes, her hands rough and strong.

"Yes, come on in! Thanks so much for bringing me lunch? I feel like I should be doing something to thank *you* for saving me yesterday!"

Lu walks toward me confidently, and pauses when she's close.

"May I?" she asks, leaning in.

"Oh yes, please," I reply as she gently kisses my cheek. I'm delighted. She smells faintly of paint and wood.

"Let me just make sure Marsha knows I'm on lunch, and then I'm all yours!" I pull away from her and lean out the door, calling to Marsha at her desk.

"Marsh? I'm on lunch; hold my calls until one—thanks!"

Marsha nods and winks at me, and I roll my eyes at her as I close the door.

"You mind if I . . ." Lu gestures to the windows.

"Oh yeah, here . . ." I snatch up the remote and press the

button to turn the glass opaque. Then I turn and sit in my desk chair, rolling it back away from my desk. I am indeed wearing a mini skirt similar to the one I was wearing yesterday, and I don't bother to straighten it as it rides up. Lu glances at my legs, and takes a step forward.

"Listen Andi. I want to take you out sometime and get to know you better, but I haven't been able to stop thinking about you in this skirt. Would you mind if we . . . started with this?"

Striding toward me, she slides between me and my desk, and drops to her knees. Her eyes are deep brown and sparkling as she gazes up at me. I have never, ever been more aroused.

"Is this ok?" She puts a hand on my knee. I'm struggling to breathe, with this gorgeous woman on her knees in front of me. Her mouth is so pretty, and her tongue sneaks out to lick her lips like she's hungry for me. I swallow hard and nod.

"Yes?"

"Yes," I breathe. "Yes, please."

She leans forward and cups her hand around my cheek, and I let her pull me toward her. We kiss, gently at first, and then deeper. She tastes like tea and cream. Then she pulls away and places her open hand on my chest, pushing me firmly back. Her fingers are rough and calloused against my skin. They catch on the fabric of my scoop-neck shirt as she rakes her hand down, exposing my black lace bra.

"God, you're so *pretty,*" she breathes, and kisses my breasts reverently. Her eyes are on my face, watching me hungrily, and I let my head fall back as I soak in her attention. "That's a good girl," she whispers against my breast as she continues kissing, her hands cupping me through my bra, her fingers finding and gently twisting my nipple through the fabric. I let myself relax into my chair, resting my head back, enjoying her touch, her breath, her careful ministrations.

When I feel her hands slide up the outside of my thighs, pushing up my skirt, I look down at her. She's resting back on her heels, her eyes closed, breathing deeply of my scent. "Mmmmm." She smiles and looks up. "You smell *divine*." Slowly, gently, she slips her hand between my legs, smiling in surprise when she feels my wetness.

"No panties?"

I smile. "I was kind of hoping . . . I mean, not that I assumed . . ."

"Oh Andi, you are *just* my type." She's gazing intently at my face as she traces a finger along my folds, sliding slightly deeper, circling my clit. I groan lightly at the pressure, and she smiles, retracing my slit, coating her finger in my wetness. Then, holding my gaze, she draws back and licks my juices off her finger. Her eyes close in ecstasy, and I feel my pussy pulse with arousal. With want.

She leans forward. "May I?"

"Please," I beg. She wraps her arms around my back and pulls us together, pressing her face deeper between my legs until she reaches my center. She gently turns her face to one side, then the other as she eases between my folds, and the pressure is absolute heaven. I feel her tongue flick out briefly, fluttering against my entrance. And again. Then she groans as she presses her tongue against me, circling my entrance, pushing firmly against my walls.

I'm breathing heavily, my shirt a mess, my skirt bunched up around my hips, as this gorgeous woman drags her tongue up to my clit, settles in deeper, and begins to suck. The push and pull of her mouth is exquisite—now fluttering like a moth, now lapping in strokes long and deep. She teases me, plays with me, takes me to the edge and then changes directions. I feel my need growing, becoming unbearable—and finally I wind my fingers through her hair with both hands and pull her firmly against me, moving my hips, grinding against her face desperately.

She reciprocates, groaning into me and gripping me tighter; our bodies meld together in this most intimate of ways as we fuck each other desperately. My thrusts grow quicker as she works me with her mouth, and then I'm coming, my pussy spasming and gushing, her face smacking noisily against my flesh.

When I finish, I push her away, gasping, rolling my chair backwards until it hits the wall.

"Oh my *god,*" I breathe. "Oh my *GOD* . . ."

She leans back on her heels, her face glistening with my juices, and grins at me, looking ecstatic and gorgeous. She wipes her face with her hands, then rubs them across the thighs of her jumpsuit, and stands. She leans over me tenderly, smoothing my skirt down over my thighs, then pulling my shirt up to cover my bra.

"Could I see you again tomorrow?" she asks, grinning at me.

I'm about to say yes, but then I realize . . . I want more of her. I want her in my bed, inside me, against me, around me . . .

"How about dinner? I'll cook for you. You know where I live."

She grins that gorgeous grin down at me as she takes my chin between her fingers and thumb.

"Sounds perfect."

THIRTEEN

Molamelons

by Mary Helen Gallucci

It isn't that I'm especially small, for a middle-aged Betorian. I'm on the petite side, it's true, but well within an average range. Nor is Sydori unusual among her kind: her head clears the stone threshold to her seaside Lymphorian home with room to spare, and her toes mostly only edge off the mattress when she tosses off her quilts on restless nights.

What is unusual is the fact that Sydori and I are, immeasurably, in love.

We met one hot summer afternoon at the market, just as the vendors were packing up to retreat from the heat of the day. I had been crossing a broad stand of molamelons—bounding from one to the next gracefully and respectfully, if in a bit of a rush—and had misjudged the integrity of one extra-soft (rotten, really) rind. There had been, I'd noticed too late, a tear in the canopy overhead, allowing one broiling dust-sparkling stream of sunlight to half-cook that particular piece of fruit. Between the weight of my backpack full of books, the goopy melon pulp suctioning my shoe—and then my ankle—

and then clinging to the hairs on my leg . . . Suffice it to say, I was *very* grateful when Sydori noticed my struggle and scooped me out.

Syd had offered to hand-deliver me home then and there, and I really *should* have taken her up on it—would have, genuinely, if there hadn't been such a mesmerizing twinkle in Syd's huge, crow-footed gray eye in that moment. Syd had so intently studied my small sticky self—my hairy, sodden legs that dangled off her palm, the goop between my wiggling toes —that I hadn't been sure if the twinkle was just some kind of condescending mirth, or possibly the seed of . . . something else? While stuck, I had thrust a hand into the melon, trying to free my shoe—and then thoughtlessly swiped my hair from my eyes, with the result that I *knew* my hair was a stringy, dripping mess of purple tangles. All I could do to remedy the situation was lick the over-sweet green goo from my fingers under Syd's inscrutable scrutiny.

"What is your name, Betorian?" Syd had asked.

"Uvalia," I'd said. "Uva."

"You . . . va," she'd repeated slowly, with a hint of wonder. I'd noticed the way her plush lips rounded, then. Almost puckered, almost . . . kissable. It had never in my life occurred to me that my name might make one ready for a kiss, and I was quite astonished by that sudden spark of clarity. What a marvelous name I'd had all along, and I'd never known!

"To the library, then, Uva?" Syd had asked, having taken keen note of my clunking backpack. The library had, in fact, been my original destination, before the mishap; and I was duly impressed by her inference.

Still, I'd said, "No," not a little scornfully. "Obviously not, looking like this?!"

Syd's warmth was utterly unaffected by my snappish tone;

if anything, her smile had broadened. "All right then . . . where would you like to be?"

I'd considered this, squinting back up to meet Syd's gaze. "Your place," I decided.

Syd then acquiesced. She thoughtfully collected bits and pieces from around her home to assemble a bath suitable to my own proportions—complete with sweet-smelling lye soaps, fine sponges for my delicate skin, and fresh water for rinsing residual pulp several times over. She brought me washcloths good as towels, apologizing that she had no appropriate robe, and promised me privacy . . . but I (bold, I know) insisted she stay.

"Please," I said, "I like you watching."

And Syd did.

The truth is, I watched Syd watching me with similar enthrallment. And after that—just in time for the afternoon siesta—I keenly invited myself into Syd's vast bed, and, well . . . by the time that first date of ours finally ended, my library books were *terrifically* overdue.

Today, some hundred moons later, is another brutally hot one, and the two of us have been lounging in the shade of our home, taking some relief in the coolness of the stone under the shade of our tree. For this very good reason, we are quite unclothed, enjoying the faintly tangy sea breeze against our skin. Syd has just cut up an especially crisp molamelon, which she'd been keeping on ice, and is just finishing reminding me —as she must every time—how cute I'd looked with molagoo in my hair.

"That seed," Syd giggles, "behind your ear, just hanging on for dear life like it couldn't get enough of you . . ."

"Oh my god, not again with the seed," I groan.

"And look where it got us," Syd continues, unperturbed. "A beautiful life, beautiful wife—"

"—Beautiful molatree," I finish with her. "Babe, you are the *sappiest*."

"Oh no, love, the *sappiest* was absolutely *you*—"

"I'm fixing that right now!" I heft a chunk of the fruit in both hands and, crawling atop Sydori, I smear a streak of its pulp up her belly, lodging the whole thing under her breast with a shove.

Syd gasps. "Uv, that—is—*cold!!*"

"You're welcome," I reply, with a self-satisfied smirk. Retrieving the chunk of fruit, I seat myself comfortably astride my wife's ribcage and take a large bite. "Mmmm," I roll my eyes theatrically, "Improves the flavor!"

Syd laughs, deep and warm and affectionate. She strokes my head with her thumb as I chew "Does it, now?"

I swat her hand away, swallowing, and then slick the chilly fruit back over the mound of Syd's breast. Around and around I swirl it over the turquoise of her rapidly-contracting areola, then heft it back to my lips for a discerning nibble. "Notes of . . . tonga nuts . . . burrberries . . . just a hint of . . . sautéed lamis root . . ."

"All that from one nipple?"

"It's the combination," I explain, indicating the fruit in my hands. "The mola brings out the finer savors."

"Aha," Syd chuckles. "Well, are you going to clean me up now, darling?"

"Clean you up?! I just started eating!" I've been exaggerating dismay, but now I reconsider. "Actually, sure, I can take care of my mess as I go."

Tossing the rest of my fruit to the side (our skumpup will be happy to slurp it up when he discovers it), I delicately lick my dainty fingers, one by one. Then I duck my head to the sticky skin just under my wife's sternum. I lap at the juice there—tiny flutters, like a goss-fly's wing—and can't help but grin when Syd jolts so hard I nearly fly off her.

"That *tickles*—Uva!!" Syd's voice has uncharacteristically risen to what could nearly be classified as a squeal, and she catches me up in her hands, squirming.

I've dug in, however, with my fingernails and the ridges of my heels, and I persist at licking and nipping, light as a feather: tiny pinpricks of my lupine teeth that only sometimes pierce the skin. I know Syd is rendered helpless under my assault for fear of breaking me, and I *never* miss a chance to use this to my own advantage. Her absolute gentleness, combined with awareness of her own strength, make her own bondage.

Indeed, Syd's hands quickly fall away to the bedsheets, which she fists in earnest. I growl my delight at the surrender.

When I've rendered her ribs *very* sparkling clean, and Syd has become quite clearly light-headed and throaty with her giggles, I pivot and head south. Juice has pooled in Syd's navel and I lap eagerly at that—it's a whole little moonglassful to me—pressing my fingertips deep into the soft flesh of her tummy. I love the give, the spongey plushness of her here; feel her flex her bed of muscles underneath as my hands and knees sink into her. Because Syd is so ticklish and yet showing *such* marvelous restraint, I spread my knees just a tad wider to improve her view of my diminutive—but now certainly *very* ripe—pussy, giving my raised hips a saucy little wiggle as I drink. Syd groans her appreciation, and then I have to sink my center into the dough of her belly for the almost-friction of it. I feel myself adding to the juices on her skin as we writhe together: Syd trying to evade the tickle-tease of my tongue's fluttering, my clit searching for pressure but deprived by her impossible softness. Finally, I surface, having licked Syd's navel dry, but having made the rest of her sticky all over again.

"Syd," I gasp, "your finger—" and, understanding, my wife sweeps a large thumb firmly over my swollen, sodden folds and needy clit, holding as I press into it greedily. Her hips roll gently under my hands in enjoyment as mine grind against her palm, appreciating the breadth and contour of her thumb as I slip against its length.

She knows I often come from this, and I would—readily— but then her palm is gone and she's nuzzling her smallest fingertip between the lips at my opening, offering without pressure. "YES," I exclaim. "*Thank* you!!" And she chuckles before humming a little as I sink back onto her. Slowly, stretching for her.

"Uva, darling," she murmurs to me, "relax. I've got you." She reaches her other hand around me to brush my nipples, pinching and plucking just a little—so soft, such tiny gestures —not enough.

"*More*," I growl, grasping at her hand roughly, and she follows, rolling the whole of my breast between her fingers. My growl becomes more ferocious with frustration, as I'm impossibly torn between sitting deeper onto her or arching up against her. "Baaaby," I whine, "I need you to *take* me."

"You're fragile, my love," she murmurs.

"I'm *not!!*" I hiss back.

"I don't want to hurt you," she says with infuriating patience. "Trust me."

I'm groaning, arching, waiting, as her slow pressure builds, then plateaus. Her fingers around my breast tighten, pinching and rolling and I hear her humming with enjoyment behind me, a smile warming her tone. "Hmmmmmmmmm." Her chest is vibrating with the low emanation, and she urges me up her torso until I feel it all through me, buzzing electric through all my nerve endings, from my lips tingling between my teeth to my clit to my toes. Now, finally, she sinks her finger into me, and I push back until she's deep enough that I'd cry out if I didn't know better—but I *cannot* let her stop now, cannot let her worry, so I dig my teeth deeper into my lip and hold my breath. "Hmmmmmmmm." My inner walls are stretching, and then squeezing, and then finally spasming so deliciously around her that I distantly hear her gasp with pleasure, the vibrations over.

I release my shriek, belated, as she pulls out of me. Then I flop, spent for the moment, onto her breast.

"You okay, love?" she asks me bemusedly.

"Yes, no thanks to you," I mutter.

"Oh, I think it's plenty of thanks to me," she chuckles, but I am distracted by the juice against my cheek.

"—And you've distracted me from my task at hand."

"How dare I," she agrees, as I fill my mouth with her nipple.

"*Mmm*," I exclaim when I come up for air. "The tonga nut flavor is much more prominent in this proportion. Syd nipple with a touch of mola juice. *Huge* fan. Now—babe, pass me another piece, please."

"Can't get enough, hm?"

"No, my curiosity is piqued. Spread for me, baby."

She passes me another melon chunk, and I move down between her parted thighs. She is melted and fragrant and the scent and sight are so heady . . . I whisper, "*Goddess*," and give one of her luscious thighs a nibble of appreciation. Then, recovering myself, I comb through the fluff of her hair until I find the pearl of her clit—it's nearly the size of my fist. I eagerly slip back the hood with one sticky hand and then plant a kiss—and a little hungry lick or two—on that beautiful nub.

"I thought—" she gasps, "You wanted the—mola flavor—"

"Palate cleanse," I say, sucking her briefly between my lips. Her clit is so sensitive, I know I should keep my teeth carefully under wraps, but it's so tempting to sink into this delicious, tender, perfect mouthful and devour her . . .

Coming up for air, I take a deep breath to clear my fantasies and remember the melon in my hand. It's warmed a bit from the heat of the room, but still a cool shock when I press it to Syd's clit, and she wriggles helplessly under my relentless application. I circle it until it's tinged green with pulp. Then I toss the melon and dive in to take care of my mess.

"God," I groan, my mouth full of her, "SO good, baby, it's like—" I lick her in broad stroke: the underside of her nub, the circumference; I slide my palm and then tongue deeper under her hood until it melts back, the bundle underneath pulsing against my lips. "I swear I bought this candy once, tasted *just* like this."

"Pussy candy?" Syd gasps incredulously, arching into me so urgently I grasp at her curls to steady myself. Her wetness has been pooling below, and now it drips slowly down my breasts and belly as I hold her close.

"*Mola*-ade, I think," I tell her. "Mmmm, sweet and tangy and juicy and just *something* . . . delectable."

"Made quite the—impression," Syd observes breathily.

"Actually, I broke a tooth on it," I recall; then I can't help but nip her SO LIGHTLY, bursting into fits of giggles when she jumps in alarm. "Sorry, sorry!!"

I pat her leg consolingly as she sits up and—she's not glaring, exactly, but she sighs at me as if to say, *Uva*, must *you*?

"Turn over for me, baby."

We have this down to a familiar dance, Syd and I: her knee there, my head here, swoop, shift, lean, rest. But for all the routine, and as much as she carefully goes out of her way to make me feel safe and comfortable, she's still my strange new world—and I intend to never run out of nooks and crannies to explore, experiments to run.

Syd settles in with her knees under her, absolutely ripe and ready for me. I stroke her damp folds, smoothing them open, tracing their creases, collecting her wetness under my fingernails, and she shudders deliciously. "Mmmm, you like that?" I ask, enjoying myself tremendously.

"Yesss," she groans in earnest.

These inner lips of hers are so engorged and slippery, I have to grasp them tightly if I want to tug on them—and I do. They stretch and pull her open, the view cavernous from my angle and her position. I inhale her scent—it wafts and pools in my belly like treblenectar—and then I breathe a warm "ahhhhhh" into her depths, relishing the way her hips jerk and roll against my face.

After petting and pulling the tender flesh around the edges of her opening a moment longer, I slide my hand—then my wrist and forearm—inside her. My fingers probe her inner front wall, spongy and slick, until I find the ridges around her G-spot. Syd hums with pleasure as I comb my fingernails over them, tickling and scratching, slipping my slender fingertips between the ridges to massage those sensitive secret crevices. Then I feel for the sensitive sponge in the center, sinking the heel of my hand into it and rubbing while she writhes and sings her encouragement in low, broken tones. "Darrrrr-ling," she purrs. "*Yeeeees.*" I brace myself to lean harder into that spot, making a fist and pressing my knuckles deeper, rolling my wrist. "Oh, that's *per*fect . . ."

Syd may be easily satisfied, but I am not ready to finish her yet. She is a hot, damp velvet sleeve as I press up past my elbow now, till I bottom out at the shoulder, hugging my cheek to the beautiful moon of her ass with my other arm. Then I'm groping for the slippery orb of her cervix; she gasps when I find it, palming it and squeezing. "Uv," she moans, "*ahh*—"

I ease up my hold just a little before she can protest, rocking it side to side, up and down, before I slip a slim thumb into the slender, viscous mouth there. Then I'm rubbing her cervix, maneuvering my hand inside her, and I have to stand on my tiptoes to watch her as her hips widen and her back arches, the side of her beautiful face pressed desperately into the pillow as she's panting. She won't tell me it's too much for her—it's not, I'm certain she can take me—but I feel her hips buck and strain away from me. She fucking loves this and I know she'll glow after, tell me I was right to persist, that I know her so well . . . so I pursue, leaning in deeper, thrusting harder.

Finally she squeezes my arm, *tight*, and I'm utterly trapped by her contracting inner muscles as she bellows at the edge of the control she holds so dear. One precipitous spasm from her, in this fix, could break my arm . . . but it's never quite happened yet. I wouldn't mind if it did. This is worth it: the way she's holding me so intimately, and so vulnerable, entirely at my whim. The absolute thrill of having her wrapped around my finger.

I crook my thumb and she comes again (or is this still the first one?) with another cry. Now I rotate my wrist, and she gasps and squeezes, her muscles pushing me out one moment and pulling me in further the next.

She's still spasming around my arm when I lean into her clit, pressing into it with my torso and grinding myself against her, since she is so carefully frozen in place. Even her breathing has stopped, and she's making little constricted grunts and gasps with the effort of her restraint. "It's okay, baby," I urge her, "loosen up, I've got you. Let go."

I feel her muscles release their death grip on my arm, still fluttering and *oh* so wet against my skin. My breasts and belly are glistening, drenched; and when I retract my arm, my fingers have wrinkled from their ablution.

"Mmmm," I murmur appreciatively, licking them. Syd has shifted to her side. Glancing up, I notice that she is smiling down at me in adoration, her hair a nest, her eyes glowing golden. "You want some?" I ask, proffering my hand.

She nods, and I move so we are face to face. Cupping my elbow in her palm, she guides my fingers into her mouth, easily sucking them clean. Then she laves my palm and wrist with her broad tongue. "I still taste a bit of the melon, actually," she tells me, eyes twinkling.

"Essence of Syd with a hint of mola," I agree.

"Not bad," she says. Then she reaches behind my ear and extracts a stray seed from my hair.

"Come, lie on my breast," she says lovingly, and I willingly oblige, resting on the most perfect pillow I have ever known.

"What shall we have for dinner?" she asks.

"Clinklin?"

"Too spicy."

"Rowshlots?"

"You nearly lost a tooth last time I made those."

"Well then," I pout, "you come up with a suggestion!"

She considers. "How about we lay here a while, eat the rest of the chilled molamelon, and then head down to the pub for a glass of niblink nectar?"

I grin up at her, nuzzling into her softness with a blissful sigh.

"That sounds as perfect as a peahorn in a plushfloom."

FOURTEEN

Home for Christmas

by Natalie Naudus

I t's December 23rd, and I'm talking to my wife on the phone.

"It just doesn't seem right!" I whine. "You should be in bed with me. Naked. Preferably sitting on my face."

"I'll be home tomorrow, Stells. And then I'd *love* to. Right after I bend you over the bathroom counter and finger you from behind. While you watch in the mirror."

"Mmmmm," I moan into the phone. "Wait until you see what I got you for Christmas."

"Stells, you've been doing so much this week. I intend to pamper *you* when I get back."

"Oh yeah?" I lie back and smile at the ceiling. "How are you gonna pamper me?"

"I'm gonna put the girls to bed when I get in."

"Ooooh, you know I love it when you talk dirty."

"And then I'm going to tidy up the house while you take a bath."

"Oh my gooood," I moan.

"And *then*. I'm going to make love to you, take some melatonin, spoon you, and get the best night's sleep I've had in weeks."

"That sounds perfect."

"I'm sorry this trip has been so long."

I pause. It has felt *so* long, but I know Mel will make it up to me when she gets home. And she's only gone because she's working. For us, her family.

"It has felt like so long," I say finally. "But it's okay, baby."

"I'll see you tomorrow, Stells. Tell the girls I can't wait to see them. I love you," she whispers into my ear through my phone.

"Goodnight, my darling," I breathe.

"Goodnight, Stells."

Ending the call, I drop the phone onto our cream-colored bedspread. I miss Melanie terribly when she's away, and the kids do too. She's such a stabilizing presence; every mundane thing feels easier and brighter when she's around. But she'll be back tomorrow. She'll be home for Christmas.

Heaving a romance-novel-worthy sigh, I shrug off the blanket and pad out into the hallway. I quietly check on Grace, who is sleeping sweetly in her princess bed—her mouth slightly open in her sleep, breathing heavily against her stuffed dinosaur. No noise from Ali's room; I check the baby monitor and see that she's sleeping soundly. I should clean the kitchen, the living room is strewn with toys and clothes, and the eternal laundry pile is waiting to be folded, but perhaps I should seize this moment . . .

I grab my vibrator from the basket on the top shelf of the closet (you never can be too careful with little ones around) and slip back into bed. Turning it on low, I ease it between my folds, and slowly slide it up to rest against my clit. I breathe deeply and think of Mel. Here in bed with me. Tomorrow. I think of her kisses, soft and slow. She presses them beneath my ear. On my chin. She sucks gently on my neck. I moan quietly as I imagine wrapping my arms around her, our breasts pressed together, her voice low and sweet in my ear.

I start to arch my back as I think of stroking the curls of her mound with my fingers. Of tracing the wetness of her slit, and gently spreading her. I moan as I hear her breath in my ear. Her panting. Her perfect soft sigh. Turning the vibrator up a bit more, I remember her mouth on my sex. My hands buried in her hair, grinding against her face, fucking her mouth, her eyes focused on me, her mouth around me. And thrusting against my vibrator, I come.

Cleaning the kitchen when the kids are up is a losing battle, but at least I have texts from Mel to keep me company.

You have no idea how much I've missed you.

Um, I think I do, if my vibrator usage is any indication.

Oh yeah? Dino Daniel been keeping you company?

Just because it's green does not make it a man, how dare you? Green is the color of Mother Earth, I'll have you know.

Ok . . . has the Green Goddess been meeting your needs?

Seriously?

Dino Deb?

> Pterasaur Thérése?

> Are you jealous of my vibrator?

> Um, absolutely. I'm thankful for her service but I plan to service my wife myself tonight.

I grin down at my phone. Gracie is pulling on my shirt. "Mommy? When will Mama be home?"

"Very soon, baby! Can you go put your Legos in the bin?"

"But *when* will Mama be home?"

"You see the time here on the stove? Can you read me the numbers?"

"Seven . . . three three?"

"That's right, baby—her flight landed over an hour ago, and she is in the taxi cab now!"

"But I've been waiting and *waiting!!*" Gracie's voice goes even more shrill and I take a deep breath, digging for patience.

"How about we go look out the window for her?"

"Yes!!" she shrieks, running to the front window and disappearing behind the curtains.

I give up on finishing the dishes, drying my hands and picking up Ali from her bouncy chair. 7:33. Almost bedtime. I feel bad for eternally counting down the hours—the minutes —until bedtime, then brush the impulse aside. I've been solo parenting all week; no need to hold on to guilt on top of the exhaustion.

I pull aside the curtain and look down at Gracie, whose hands and nose spare pressed against the glass, joining the host of tiny greasy handprints and nose prints already smearing the window. I should clean the window again. Or maybe I should just give up cleaning it . . .

A cab pulls up to the curb, and Gracie is shrieking,

dancing her way to the door. And there, climbing out of the car, is my Melanie. She retrieves her carry-on from the trunk, and then she's climbing the steps to our stoop, throwing open the door . . .

"Mama's home!" she calls. And Gracie is squealing and hugging her and kissing her, and Ali is kicking her little feet and smiling her single-toothed smile, and I'm leaning over the curly heads of our daughters to kiss my wife.

"My babies!" She smiles, and fuck if it doesn't feel like the sun shining after weeks of rain. I feel myself tearing up, and I'm sniffing back tears. My wife is home.

I'm just getting out of the bath when Mel pokes her head in the bathroom. "I've still got it!" She beams.

"They're both asleep? Seriously??"

"Hey, what can I say, I've got the magic touch." She salutes me with her glass of bourbon.

"That's so unfair, it's been a struggle almost every night!"

"Hey, no more trips for a while. Mama's here for all the foreseeable bedtimes."

I walk over to her, wrapped in my towel, and kiss her. She wraps her arms around me. Slides her warm hands down my back. She tastes like whiskey and home.

"Why don't you shower," I say, "and I'll meet you in bed."

"Yes, ma'am." She grins at me. "Should I bother getting dressed?"

"Only if you want to watch me take your clothes off again."

"I mean, I know you find my sports bra and boxers irresistible."

"Um, you *know* I do." We slide against each other through the narrow door frame, pausing for another kiss. "Ask if I'm ready before you come out, okay? I got you a little surprise."

I towel-dry my hair, listening to the gentle patter of the shower. Heading to the closet I pull out the gift I ordered, and lovingly put it on.

"You ready?"

"Yeah, come on out!"

Mel comes out of the bathroom wrapped in a towel, her hair dripping onto her soft shoulders. She freezes when she sees me, and I feel suddenly shy, snatching up a pillow. "Is it too much?"

"Babe."

"Is it??"

"Stella. Let me see you." She gently pushes the pillow down and leans back to admire me. She traces her finger down the straps of the bra, skimming over the thick red ribbon tied over my breasts.

"I saw the bow and just thought it would be a fun Christmas gift. You get to unwrap me! But if you aren't into it, I can totally just . . ."

"Stella. I love it. I love you. Baby. You are just . . ." She leans in and kisses me, so gently, tipping my chin toward her. I melt into her touch, sighing against her lips as she drops her towel and wraps me in her arms, pressing her soft body to mine. My hands travel around her, sinking my fingers into the gentle rolls of her back, the plush curves of her hips.

Mel playfully shoves me onto the bed. I've been here with her a thousand times before, but she still takes my breath away. The way she pauses to caress my body with her eyes. The way she sighs and whispers, "Holy hells, Stells . . ." as she climbs over me.

"May I?" she asks, gently tugging on the bow covering my breasts.

"Please." I smile up at her. She unties the bow, the silk rasping against my skin, and then I feel cool air on my nipples. She leans over me and kisses me, her own nipples skimming across my chest. Lovingly, she kisses her way along my collarbone and lower, and as she takes my nipple in her mouth, she reaches a hand up to hold my neck.

Her fingers are gentle on my throat and her mouth is warm on my nipple, and I'm gasping gently when suddenly, she sits up. Her weight grinds on my hips as she reties the bow.

"It's Christmas Eve, Stells; I can't open my present until Christmas Day."

"*Mel!*" I laugh. "You cannot seriously . . ."

"Nope!" She has that stupid smirk on her face, mostly serious with a cheerful curl at the edges. "Nope, Santa would be *very* disappointed."

"Mel!" I'm crying, I'm laughing so hard. I wriggle out from under her and push her down, straddling her. I hold her arms above her head.

"God, I missed you," I breathe.

"My Stells." She smiles softly at me. I sit up and begin untying the ribbon again. I feel her eyes on me, and relish the pressure of her gaze. The beauty of being desired and loved and safe.

She reaches her hands up and cups my breasts, her palms warm against my skin. She gently pinches my nipples and I gasp. "Merry Christmas to me," Mel says softly as she reaches around and undoes the clasp of my bra, slipping it off my shoulders. I lean over her and kiss her. Gently at first, and then deeper, our breath quickening and mingling, her hands in my hair, on my back, gripping my ass, pushing aside my panties to dip her finger into my wetness. I stand quickly and slip them off, tossing them on the floor . . . and then I'm back on her, our pubic hair gently rasping together, and she's so soft and so warm and so mine.

I gasp as she eases a finger inside me. "God, I missed you," I whimper.

"You feel like heaven," she moans as she slides in a second finger. I rock my hips, riding, grinding down on her knuckles. Her eyes meet mine as I feel her curl her fingers inside me, rubbing, stroking, turning. I whimper when she pulls them out.

"Lean on the headboard, Stells," she commands me. I climb off her, leaning against the wall, obediently bending over and baring myself to her. As she sinks two fingers into me from behind, her other arm wraps around me, her breasts on my back and her breath against my neck.

"Melanie. Mel," I gasp gently.

"God, you are so beautiful. I adore you," she whispers into my ear. "Can you take another finger?" she asks.

"Mmm." I nod, leaning over further, opening myself to her. I gasp as her fingers spread me wider. I feel myself accepting her, welcoming her into me. Her other hand travels my body: gently squeezing my neck, playing with my nipples, finding my clit and circling. All the while she's warm and real at my back, thrusting and grunting as her fingers explore me, feel me, know me, and I'm near tears at the intimacy and beauty of being with her again.

"*Stella*," she moans into my ear. "My Stells. My darling wife. God, you feel so good."

I whimper as her fingers continue to thrust into me.

"You are such a good girl. My sweet girl," she whispers, and I feel my core tighten. The sensations are overwhelming, pushing me over the edge.

"*Mel!*" I gasp as I come on her hand, and she holds me close, stroking me through my orgasm.

"Mel, baby," I gasp as I fall onto the bed, boneless. "God, I missed that. I missed you."

"My Stells," she says tenderly, cradling my head with her arm, lying beside me. She gently lifts my hair off my face, and kisses my sweaty forehead. She looks so blissful. So proud and perfect. I touch her nipple and she gasps, and that noise from her is as pleasurable as the orgasm she just gave me.

And then I'm on her, kissing her face, her neck, then gently biting her ears the way she likes. Her breasts are small and perfect, her nipples dark and delicious on my tongue. I kiss worshipfully across her belly, each hill and valley decadent perfection.

"*Stella,*" she gasps. "*Baby.*"

I lie down beside her, and gesture. "Come here, my love. Please fuck my face. Please."

She climbs on top of me, straddles my head with her powerful thighs, and slowly lowers herself onto me. She's warm and wet and fuck if her pussy on my face isn't the best feeling in the world. I look up at her, her eyes glazed with desire. Her fingers are buried in my hair, and she knows I want her as much as she wants me. She lowers herself further, and she spreads around my mouth.

My nose is buried in her curls and her lips are against mine. I slip my tongue into her entrance, and her moan vibrates down through her body. I moan in response as I trace her entrance with my tongue, relishing the feel of her, the taste of her. She pulls my head against her tighter, and I gently suck on her clit, the way I know she likes. And then she's grinding against me, fucking my mouth, her head falling back, her cries and moans filling me with pleasure. I eat her out with the passion of all the nights I'd missed her. I moan against her and rock my head from side to side, and thrill when she goes quiet, freezing in her thrusting. Then she gives a few uncontrolled, jerky shudders as she comes.

"*Stella!*" she gasps, and falls limp beside me. We tangle together, in a magical bubble of warmth and sweat and the sweet smell of our bodies. She kisses me tenderly.

"Wow." She smirks. "I taste amazing."

"You do," I agree, tracing a finger across her cheek. Her leg is between mine, and I start gently grinding on her, feeling my wetness slide against her skin. "More orgasms please?" I whisper. I feel her smile against my lips.

"Absolutely."

FIFTEEN

Ice Time

by Natalie Naudus

I'm finalizing the lines for this weekend's hockey tournament when Katia bursts into my office.

"Figure skaters are not getting enough ice time!"

Her ponytail is as high as ever, her dark hair slicked back immaculately against her head. I shuffle my papers with a sigh, and turn to give her my full attention.

"Whoa there, Kate, whose name is on the door? Last time I checked, it was mine, as *I* am the director of skating here at the rink."

"It's *Katia*, not 'Kate,'" she corrects me haughtily. "And if you are the director of skating, that includes the figure skaters, not just the hockey players. The Free Skate this afternoon was too crowded for the skaters to work their programs, but you"—she points at me accusatorially—"have three Stick-and-Shoots scheduled, and those are almost empty."

"Katia, we have to give the 10U and 8U players their own ice time; it's dangerous to have 7-year-olds out there with high schoolers practicing their slap shots."

"This is the last Free Skate before the competition, and my

skaters should be able to practice their program fully!" Katia's face is growing red with frustration. She's wearing a coat from being in the rink, but it's warm in my office. She unzips it as she continues to scold me, revealing her tight V-neck shirt underneath, and I have to fight to keep my eyes on her face. "With nearly thirty skaters on the ice this last session, it doesn't give everyone an opportunity to run their program!"

"Thirty skaters? I hadn't realized it was quite that crowded."

"This is what I'm telling you! It's unacceptable!"

The lights in my office flicker, and then go out as the electricity in the building whines to a halt. I wonder for a brief, ridiculous second if Katia's anger has blown a circuit. But then I hear voices in the rink, loud and urgent, and realize we've lost power.

"Must be the summer heat wave." I push back from my desk and stand. "We've got to get everyone off the ice."

"If this junk heap of a rink doesn't have a generator and that ice melts, I'm going to lose a full day of students tomorrow—"

"Calm your tits, Kate—sorry, *Katia*. Let's get the building cleared, and then I can get the generator running. Would you mind checking the locker rooms, and I'll clear the ice and the lobby?" She glares at me so angrily that I'm reminded of the moment during a game when someone is about to ditch their gloves and start throwing punches, but she shakes it off and storms out of my office.

"We aren't finished here, Martin."

"It's Martín!" I yell after her, but she doesn't slow her pace as she storms down the darkened hallway toward the locker rooms.

I open the door to the south rink, and the cold smell of the ice greets me, a bit stiller than usual with the shut-off airflow. The exit signs glow brightly in the dark, lighting my way to the rink door.

"Hey folks! Seems like we've lost power; the Public Skate is just about over, anyhow! Please return your rentals if you have them and make your way to the exit!"

Skaters make their way to the door, some kids laughing, one crying and worried. I verify at a glance that their parent is with them, and then head down the hallway to the north rink. It's a bit lighter in there, some high windows brightening the dark space. The Stick-and-Shoot players are still at it like nothing is amiss, and I have to yell loudly to be heard.

"Hey kids, the power is out! Please clear out as quickly as you can, the rink is closed for the day!"

"Aw, come on, Coach, it's fun skating in the dark!" Garrett, a lanky high schooler, calls to me.

"I'm not getting my ass sued because one of you trips in the dark and breaks your neck! You heard me, get off the ice and clear out! And check your email before practice tomorrow; unless you hear from me, the power is back on and we practice as usual!"

By the time I make it to the front desk, the public skaters are filing out into the hot summer evening. I check with Clark in the pro shop: he's started up the generator and is heading out early. I have Melissa and Jill at the front desk call the coaches whose teams were supposed to meet tonight to cancel their ice time, and then I lock the doors behind them.

When I return to the south rink, the quiet and calm greets me like an old friend. I've always loved the rink when the power goes out. Sure, we lose out on the business hours, but the stillness of the building, the dark and the cold, are so peaceful that I can't resist. I grab my skates from the office, lace them up, and take a few laps on the empty ice. Its crunch against my blades soothes me as I push myself a bit, picking up speed, practicing some tight turns.

Then, suddenly, Katia is in front of me and I come to a quick hockey stop, spraying snow all up her black pants and coat. She sustains her haughty stance, and then, somehow maintaining her posture of authority, she reaches up and wipes the snow from her face, shaking it off her hands disdainfully.

"Sorry K, I didn't see you there. I thought you headed out with everyone else!"

"We weren't done talking," she says primly, returning her hands to her hips. She's taller in her skates—which is to say, still not very tall at all. She's a good deal shorter than me, but with her perfect posture, I somehow feel like I'm looking up at her.

"Oh yeah . . . join me for an emergency-exit-sign-lit stroll around the rink?"

"If you are flirting with me, *director*—"

"Just a friendly skate. We just skate and talk. I promise."

She glares at me, and I'm sure she's going to refuse. But then, with a huff, she takes off across the ice. I try not to grin as I catch up to her.

"So, I see what you're saying, and I'll add some more Free Skates," I offer. "But if you need extra ice time before a competition, can you let me know in advance? I'm happy to schedule the ice time, I just need to know in time to plan the schedule."

Katia looks briefly surprised, and then nods curtly. She's so effortlessly stern, I find it adorable, but I pull myself together and finish explaining.

"This is the first time I've heard about it. It's always a balance trying to keep the figure skaters and hockey players in enough ice time, and I had seen some pretty empty Free

Skates last month, so I thought it made sense to replace some Free Skates with Stick-and-Shoots."

"Last month was unusually light; lots of kids were on vacation." She spins effortlessly and continues backwards, facing me as she talks. "But yes, I'll email you the competition dates for the rest of the year."

"Would it help to have a Free Skate just for your students the Thursday before a competition?"

"Of course, but I don't want to impose . . ."

"No, it's not a problem. I know you haven't been here long, but I do try to be a reasonable director."

We slow to a stop by the benches, and Katia leans an elbow on the plexiglass.

"I see that now, and I appreciate it. I'm sorry if I came on too harsh. I'm just used to having to fight for what the figure skaters need."

"Hey, I understand," I say, mirroring her lean on the plexiglass. "But I was a figure skater first; I'll always have your back. Just tell me what you need."

"You were a figure skater?" She quirks a perfectly arched brow in surprise.

"Hard to imagine, right? But yeah, I was all in . . . until I grew a foot in middle school. When I realized I was going to be closer to six foot than five, and I knew I wanted to keep skating, I switched to hockey. I sucked ass at puck handling, but I put in a lot of work and . . . well, here I am."

"You know, I can see it," Katia says. "Your edges—you use them better than most hockey players."

It's my turn to be surprised. "Really?"

"I've seen you teaching." She almost smiles at me. "You skate with power."

I'm blushing and looking down, and suddenly her white

figure skates are toe to toe with my black hockey skates. When I look up, she's right in front of me.

"You are full of surprises, director Martín," she says gently, looking up at me. I've never seen her like this, soft and open, and when she grabs me by the collar of my coat and rises on her toe picks to press her lips to mine, I'm so surprised I glide back away from her, breaking the kiss.

"I'm so sorry," she says in a rush, turning away, "I must have misread things, I apologize!" And then she's skating away, and I'm chasing after her. I'm catching her hand and pulling her in and then we are kissing and spinning and I don't know which way is up or down, only that her lips are warm and her nose is cold, and we are locked together in this perfect, breathless moment.

When we break apart, she exhales heavily, her breath glowing in frosty curls. "Come with me," she orders, taking me by the hand, and I follow. She pulls me into a dark locker room, and then she's kissing me again, pushing me roughly against the door, her delicate hands gripping my hair, my chin, my neck. I've never kissed a girl so small and femme, but so powerful that I can feel the strength of her body in her every movement. She places her forearm against my chest, pinning me against the door, and slides her other hand under my waistband.

"May I?" she asks, and I nod, speechless. And then her hand is sliding into my pants, into my boxers, her delicate fingers brushing my folds and she's kissing my neck hungrily, desperately, nipping at my chin, pulling my coat open to nuzzle at my collar bones.

"Katia, I had no idea," I pant. "You're so beautiful, but I didn't dare hope . . ."

"You can call me Kate," she interrupts with a smirk, "and I want to taste you. Please."

"Yes," I whisper, "if you want to . . ."

"I want you." She straightens to her full height, reaching just about my chin, and glares up at me with that flash of defiance I've come to know so well.

"I just thought you . . . well, I thought you hated me? Or at least really *disliked* me . . ."

"I don't hate you." She puts a finger on my lips. "And I've been *dreaming* about putting my mouth on you, so if the feeling is at all mutual . . ."

"It is." I nod. "But Katia—Kate. I don't . . . I don't come easily. And never with a partner. I don't want you to be disappointed . . ."

"Do you still enjoy sex?" she demands.

"I . . . yes, I do."

"Then just tell me when you want me to stop, okay?"

"Okay," I breathe.

A slow grin creeps across her face—the first one I've ever seen from her—as she kneels in front of me, tugging down my pants. Then she leans forward, nuzzling into my sex, and breathes deeply. I shiver at the image. This gorgeous, arrogant woman, on her knees for *me*, hungry for *me*. And then those fiery eyes meet mine as she opens her mouth and I feel her warmth, the glide of her tongue, the pressure of her lips. Her eyes roll back in ecstasy and she moans against me, and it's all I can do to stay upright.

She grabs my hand and places it on her head firmly, and I respond to her request. I wind her ponytail around my fist and pull her to me, grinding against her, fucking her gorgeous face as the sucks me eagerly, desperately.

"Kate," I moan, "God you are so fucking *gorgeous*. You are just . . . oh my *god*."

She groans in pleasure and continues to work me with her mouth. My hips buck involuntarily and I worry I've been too rough, but she moans with pleasure and wraps her arms around me, pulling me in closer, pressing her face in deeper. Her eyes are so big and beautiful as they gaze up at me, she's blinking so slowly in her bliss, and I'm overcome with the image, the sensations as she worships me with her mouth.

And then, suddenly, it's all too much, and I push her away, my legs trembling, my sex aching.

"I'm sorry, I just . . . I can't anymore, it's just too sensitive . . ."

She smiles up at me and *licks her lips*, rising from her knees, pulling my pants back around my waist. "Thank you," she says sweetly, lifting on her toe picks to plant a kiss on my lips. She tastes salty and sweet, and she smells like me.

"Buy me dinner, and then we'll continue this at my place?" She takes my hand and pulls me along, and I follow. My god, do I follow.

SIXTEEN

The Art of Soup

by Mary Helen Gallucci

*A*strid had grown really quite bored of her team, several of whom had turned out to be not only pitiful at subterfuge, but constitutionally unable to blend in. Her lookout, Jem, was particularly hopeless, and as tempting as it was to just let him be carted off by the first nefarious thug whose eye he tripped, her team's integrity and secrets were at stake. So, today—like most days, lately—Astrid was employing her own eagle eyes, lurking hazily in a shadowed alley behind the old hostel where their next mark was meant to arrive . . . sometime this month. The hostel was dingy and deserted (why would a man whose head was worth so much lay it on a pillow so likely to be infested with mites?) and the alley was as well. It was absolute tedium.

Which was why she was utterly *tickled* when what felt like a cold rod sidled up along her ribs. A gloved hand slid over her mouth and a cool voice breathed low in her ear, "I believe you have something that belongs to me."

She knew that voice, and the slight bite of that particular blade. It would, of course, have been a simple matter to dissolve into the shadow and reappear across the alley. But Sora would have expected as much, so it would hardly have been enough to catch her off guard. Besides, Astrid didn't mind the feeling of being bound in the other woman's leather-clad arms a moment longer than strictly necessary. She hummed, then sank her sharp teeth into the glove, and the hand dropped from her mouth to clasp across her shoulders instead. "Your . . . attention?" Astrid guessed, folding down her delight into something she hoped sounded merely coy.

The arms stiffened with a creak, and Astrid bit back a smirk. A little of her blood dripped down the blade lodged under her rib, but only slowly. "Hardly," Sora hissed.

Astrid's laugh was a touch high, her diaphragm being restricted as it was. "Oh, I asked it like a question, but it wasn't one, really. You're here, aren't you? Or perhaps my boredom got the better of me and I dreamed you up?" She tipped her head. "Wouldn't be the first time . . ."

She felt Sora's breath hitch, just faintly, and she couldn't suppress her giggle, though the patter of her blood dripping onto the dusty paving stones quickened abruptly. "No," Sora said. "You kept my best star."

"Your *what?*"

She had meant to tease, but quickly regretted it; Sora's blade-arm flexed to slice just as Astrid regretfully dissipated from her embrace and approached again from an adjacent shadow. Sora whirled on her. "That belonged to my father. There isn't another throwing star like it, and I have far too many enemies to be able to afford giving away weapons as keepsakes."

Astrid shrugged. "Maybe just kill them faster?"

Sora circled, angling to corner Astrid into the sunlit side of the alley. "Return it now, or I'll take that advice."

"If it's so important, why didn't you kill me with it when you threw it?"

Sora gritted her teeth. "I didn't think you deserved to die. *Then.*"

"Why, Sora!" Astrid clasped her chest. "But if you were so endeared to me, you might have told me so!"

"Do you have it on you?"

"Of course I do! Why would I come for a mark without my best throwing star?"

"*My* best throwing star. Well then, where is it?"

"I suppose you'll need to find it."

"You'll pull a knife on me if I come so close."

"I would never! . . . I mean, yes, of course I would, but I promise to restrain myself while you search for your star."

Sora huffed, exasperated. "You couldn't just hand it to me?"

"I truly couldn't."

Growling, Sora patted down Astrid's thighs (only knives there), the small of her back, the cups of her brassiere. "You are lying to me!"

Astrid giggled with delight. "Why would I lie to you when the truth is so much fun?"

"Where is it, then?"

"What?"

"My *star*, you daft cow."

"Oh—the *star*, yes: that is underneath my pillow."

"Why is it *there?!*"

"In case you came looking for it! Seemed like a good place to make you look. Though we really should find some dinner first; are you hungry? I'm famished."

"So you DID lie to me."

As much as Astrid had enjoyed toying with her attacker (she wished very much that she could think of her as *prey*, but somehow the dignity of her opponent precluded that preferred paradigm), she cast an eye to the angle of the sun, and then relented. "Oh! I see the confusion. Yes, I did. Now, if you'll just follow me . . ."

Sora was far too wise to actually follow, of course. She was, in fact, implementing the beginning of a plan of attack that would have certainly taken Astrid's life, had Astrid's posse not arrived at the designated place at the designated time and, instead of collecting the original mark or at least some booty, been obliged instead to take Sora away in bondage. It seemed like a boring conclusion to the most interesting thing that had happened all month . . . until Astrid remembered that there were as yet no further plans for what to *do* with Sora, in bondage.

When the two reconvened, Sora was roped by the wrists in a makeshift way (though it was really quite effective; Astrid had to give props to her team's ingenuity) and hooked to the wall in a damp little cellar below the old distillery. It was not, by any measure, the most effective use of resources; as far as they knew, nobody had noticed the warrior woman's absence, so they weren't sure what (if anything) she'd end up being worth —hopefully not swiftly slit throats. But she seemed worth keeping alive, anyway.

Jem had been taking a bowl of steaming leek broth precariously down the creaky ladder when Astrid intercepted and usurped the duty. Her prisoner, her problem, she'd said. She'd snuck a few green leaves and a dollop of cream into the broth before taking to the ladder herself. No sense killing the woman, after all. Not by starvation. There were plenty more satisfying ways to accomplish it.

When she approached, Sora flexed her long fingers over her head and laughed. "Not quite what I had in mind, but I knew you'd take me up on it eventually."

Astrid narrowed her eyes. "Take you up on—what?"

"Getting soup, of course! This venue is a bit subpar; I'd have taken you somewhere a little more . . . refined."

"You'd have taken me to the afterlife," Astrid scoffed.

"The Afterlife Cafe in Dregstown isn't much, but it'd top this. I was thinking someplace more like . . . The Little Quail."

"You have a base there?" Astrid was intrigued: this had not been billed as an espionage kidnapping, but if it turned out useful on that front, this could help justify the bowl of soup to her team.

Sora huffed. "You think I'd tell *you*, if I did? For *lunch*, you nearsighted fox. Are you going to free my hands so I can drink that?"

"Hardly," Astrid scoffed, collecting a spoonful of broth and blowing the steam from it with a cool breath. "We'd be thrown out of a respectable joint like that before first blood was even drawn. Open."

Sora gave her a scathing look before parting her lips wide enough to accept the spoon. Her tongue started at the heat of the broth, causing a bit to dribble over her lip and down to her chin.

Astrid just watched the liquid path left by that droplet closely. She had to lean in to see it, given the scarcity of light that leaked into the cellar. "Are you going to attend to that?" she asked quietly, finding herself inches from the other woman's face. When Sora jerked at her creaky bonds by way of response, Astrid burst into a fit of giggles. "Oh, I'm *so* sorry!" she laughed, and then rose on her tiptoes and lapped at the droplet with one swift flick of her tongue. "My mistake."

Sora's open mouth was steaming. "More," she panted.

"So you *do* like my cooking! I'm flattered. . . . Or?" Astrid raised a single coy eyebrow. "Perhaps it's my tongue that you like?" She leaned in again, breathing so close to Sora's neck that she could feel goosebumps prickling along it. "Oh, Sora," she murmured. "You are in *desperate* need of a wash. So inelegant, allowing yourself to steep in your own"—the tip of her tongue darted out for a taste—"juices for . . . days, is it?"

Sora's breath had hitched in her throat, and now her bosom was heaving against Astrid's to compensate. Astrid smiled against her neck, then flattened her tongue to give the other woman a long, feline lick up to her earlobe. "So, which is it you like?" she purred, "my cooking, or . . ."

"S-soup," Sora rasped without hesitation.

Astrid stepped back abruptly, and glared. "I see," she snapped. "Open."

Sora met her hard gaze and acquiesced, parting her lips.

"Tip your head back this time, you dingy donkey, if you don't want a nursemaid to have to sop you up!"

Sora's eyes narrowed before she tipped her chin up, her long throat glistening.

Astrid lifted the steaming bowl . . . and poured it, slowly, careful not to spill a drop, straight down the writhing woman's gullet.

A few days later, after they had both cooled off quite a bit, Astrid returned and approached Sora with yet another bowl.

Actually, this one was substantially bigger, and it was a wonder how the lithe wisp of a girl had managed getting it down the ladder intact.

"What now?" Sora's voice still rasped, throat a bit less raw but perhaps beginning to scar over.

"I'm here for your bath," Astrid told her. "My cell has been complaining that it smells like something died in here. . . . Which is entirely possible; this place hasn't been fumigated in years. But I thought it would be a good idea to rule out the possibility that you rolled in dung on your way here."

"I smell fine."

"You'll smell better in a few minutes."

"And I suppose you're here to watch?"

"Oh no, my dear viper, I'm here to wash you. How could you possibly do it, all tied up like that?"

The corner of Sora's cracked lips crooked a tiny sliver of a smirk. "You'd be surprised."

Astrid cocked her head in sincere curiosity. "What might *that* mean?"

"The hubris," Sora chuckled to herself. "All right, then, go ahead."

This gave Astrid uncharacteristic pause. But after a moment of challenging eye contact, she set down her bowl, dipped and wrung out her rag, and then approached the other woman. She began at her chest, which felt accessible, being conveniently located at eye level. Astrid ran the rag over Sora's collarbone, her shoulders, her neck, and then into the cleavage between her leather-clad breasts. Hm. She was not going to get far without ridding the woman of her combat suit.

Astrid's own coverings were far more casual; the deserted building she occupied with her little crew was as much a home to her as anything, and she hadn't dressed for certain combat as Sora had. In fact, she hadn't even dressed for the incidental combat one might expect day-to-day, lounging in a borrowed home. She had dressed for . . . well, *this* precise type of combat. She'd worn only a black leather bustier and matching underpants, with the thigh-high leather hose she needed for knife concealment, and the tall boots needed to bring her even into range of her target's eye-level.

Astrid instinctively reached for the knife at her thigh; the notion of cutting the leather from Sora's body sounded *delicious*, and she was itching to do it . . . but that would leave Sora with nothing to wear. A stark-naked hostage would be a distinct tactical disadvantage should the need arise to relocate —or tactfully negotiate a price for her release.

Before re-sheathing the blade, she checked Sora's face for any sign of fear. A hint of anxiety, even, would be exquisite on those sharp, hardened features. . . . But very much to her disappointment, there was no such sign of weakness. Sora's eyes might have been *gleaming* just a touch, in fact.

Astrid flicked the edge of the knife with her fingernail—a delightful metallic *ziing*—and bared her own sharp dogteeth, daring the other woman to flinch. Unfortunately, she paid no such favor. Sora's impassivity—bemusement, even?—caused Astrid to reconsider her resolve not to cut the suit off, out of sheer annoyance—and maybe give Sora's too-thick skin a little slice, just for a pick-me-up. Perhaps there, between her breasts . . .

Astrid slowly drew just the tip of her knife up the leather corset from belly to bust, till it dropped into the hollow there. In the silence of the dusty little dungeon, she thought she could almost hear the beating heart she so longed to torment . . . or maybe that was only her own blood rushing loudly in her ears. She pressed in just a bit, until a ruby red drop of blood trickled down the other woman's sternum, disappearing beneath the stiff fabric. Astrid was surprised at how easy that was, in fact. Perhaps Sora's skin was thinner than she'd let on.

Tearing her eyes from the dripping scarlet trail into the shadow, Astrid noticed Sora's chin tipped down, breath coming hot and heavy, fogging the blade. Astrid was gratified. She had earned this small obeisance, surely. She could make Sora feel—*something.* If it wasn't sheer terror, all the better. She did know of *one* thing more diverting than fear.

Now that Astrid looked closely, she saw that there was a thin leather thong lacing up the front of the other woman's bodice. That, Astrid swiftly calculated, was expendable, placing no financial burden on her crew should it require replacement. With a flick, she snapped through the top stitch, revealing just a single glimpse more of the drip of blood.

Emboldened, she ripped through several more stitches with the tip of her blade, until the seam gave way and loosened itself, releasing its bind down toward Sora's navel. There was one more layer of cloth stuck against her skin: a thin undergarment with a patch now stained a deep sticky crimson, and frayed already from Astrid's knifework.

While Sora's stupid face remained stubbornly impassive, her nipples stood distinctly at attention beneath the single woven layer. Astrid found herself very, *very* satisfied by this physical admission of investment in her actions—all the more because she'd inspired a mutiny. Sora's body, disciplined and battle-hardened as it was, breaking to betray the rigid governance of her mind. Just for Astrid. She felt the power they were giving her. And felt very . . . ingratiated, to those rebellious nipples.

She was fully prepared to demonstrate her appreciation for their uprising. She gave one of them an agreeable little nip, tempered by the cloth. The way the material quivered slightly when she released it shot a thrill to her core. The stony Sora she knew would never *jiggle*. This was too good.

After Astrid's knife had encouraged the corset the rest of the way open, she dropped it; it had done its job. Bracing her palms against the wall behind Sora, under the woman's upstrung arms, she snagged the thin material of the undergarment between her sharpest teeth. Then she *yanked.*

Sora gasped, her fists clenching around the creaking leather that held them as her body jerked with the sudden force. When she looked down, Astrid was grinning toothily and shoving the layers of rent material back over Sora's shoulders, framing her bare chest.

Astrid was pleased to have Sora in a double-bind: wrists tied to the wall as before, but now also her upper arms caught up in her own once-skin-tight garments. If those wrists were free, Astrid's mind couldn't help but calculate, Sora could certainly have her in a headlock instantly, the taut cloth at Sora's arms down around her own neck—a fatal advantage. Astrid would be smothered there, immobilized against Sora's supple bare breasts, in moments. She could use her ability to vanish, of course, but would she have the sense to? What a way to go. . . . It was a risk Astrid was willing to take.

And besides, Sora's wrists *weren't* free. She *belonged* to Astrid. Supple bare breasts and all.

And gods, if Astrid had delighted in the taut attention of those eager nipples before, she luxuriated in them now. Before her eyes, they strained to abandon all loyalty to Sora and *worship* her, Astrid, as her own devoted acolytes. She purred her acceptance, pinching them with both hands. "Mine," she murmured with satisfaction. But when she thought to check, she saw that Sora simply averted her eyes. There was no avoiding this, Astrid was determined. She pinched harder, till Sora's teeth ground together. She pulled. Sora's back arched deliciously away from the wall as her sensitive skin stretched. "*Mine*," Astrid insisted.

"Ha," Sora finally uttered throatily. It was obviously an attempt at defiance, but to Astrid's sensitive ears, it missed its mark by miles. Sora's expression was strained, jaw locked, brows high on her broad forehead, breaking a sweat. Astrid noticed the other woman's thighs squeezing together, and she knew she'd won.

"Ha!" Astrid crowed, releasing Sora's nipples from her grasp and, as they sprung back, flushed and tender, she gave them each a generous, appreciative lick. Sora's full bronzed breasts—so statuesque against her chiseled torso—were astonishingly warm and pliant against her tongue . . . and now, they glistened. Astrid felt confident that those weren't the only parts of Sora that were becoming wet. She herself certainly was. She could smell it.

Which was, she suddenly recalled, her purpose in being there. Her . . . *alleged* purpose. The bath. Of course, this had been the game all along. The washbowl had been an excuse— a diversion. She'd gotten a taste of Sora's skin with that dribble of soup and had been mad with the need for more. What Astrid had in mind was driven by hunger more than hygiene. But she could keep playing the game.

She picked up her rag from the bowl and wrung it out. The water had cooled significantly, and when she pressed it to Sora's breast, the other woman gasped audibly. Goosebumps broke out across her chest. She shuddered as Astrid swiped the rag over her skin, cleaning off that streak of blood down between her breasts, then her torso. Her trembling was spectacular.

Next, Astrid pulled the other woman's hips away from the wall, giving her access to wash Sora's back under the loosened layers, and grinding herself against Sora quite shamelessly in the process. Sora, as ever, held firm; and for once, Astrid was gratified by that refusal to shrink back. She had to stand on tiptoe to align her center against the thick leather seam at Sora's, where the pant legs stitched together, but once she did, the friction was perfect. She wondered how Sora got anything done with this rough bulge running against her mound. The material between her own legs was so thin as to not matter at all, and the rag slopped damply to the floor as Astrid gripped Sora's ass tightly with both hands, growling.

"Look at you," Sora ground out with difficulty. "You're a pathetic dog. I don't want your—fleas."

This brought Astrid out of her rhythm and she slowed, forcing a laugh. "Oh, you do, though!"

"Prove it," Sora dared her, the huskiness of her voice betraying her attempt at a scoff.

"I will." Astrid grinned. "Gladly." She took half a step back, kicked one of Sora's legs out from under her with a thick boot, and then, bracing her weight against that open thigh, slithered slender fingers under the lacing at the other woman's mound. Sora's head fell back with a grimace as impudent fingertips probed through curls and crevices, Astrid's knuckles straining against the leather.

Only a muscle at Sora's jaw twitched when Astrid's finger slid inside her.

"It's a pot of creamed soup in here," Astrid hissed in Sora's ear, triumphant.

"You fed me yours," Sora breathed. "Mine's better."

"Oh you *want* me to test it?" Astrid's long finger stirred in slow circles.

"I already know," Sora retorted. "Eat what you want."

Taken aback by the new direction Sora's confidence had taken, Astrid could only work out one proper contrary course of action. Well, two. Option A: she *could* walk away from the woman then and there.

"Shall I leave you dripping," she offered sweetly, if a bit breathlessly, "into the lacing of that seam? Helpless to finish yourself with your hands out of reach?" That *would* be punishment, for sure. It wasn't the kind Astrid had wanted, but perhaps she should back off and substantiate the threat, just to see if it might crack Sora's austere composure. She suspected it wouldn't, that grim old tortoise.

Sora thrust against her hand, boldly, just once. "If you walk away," she uttered, "You'll be the one who needs the cold bath."

Gods damn her, it wasn't untrue. Option B, then.

With a frustrated little roar, Astrid yanked her hand from Sora's pants, then grabbed her knife off the floor. She slid the blade in where her hand had been, flat against the other woman's pussy. Then she twisted it, so the edge sliced cleanly through the damp, sticky lacing. As her knife clattered to the floor, Astrid knelt and roughly yanked the material down to Sora's thighs, ignoring the way it bit into the soft flesh there.

Astrid grasped the dark curls on Sora's outer lips, spreading them before herself. "Ah, Sora," she purred. "But you are *so* soft, and wet, and"—she rolled her thumb over the woman's clit, gratified by the tremor that shook through her— "and *vulnerable*." She basked in this for a moment, then added: "I could just . . ." and flicked her clit with an aggressive little *snap*: at which Sora finally, *finally*, cried out.

Smugly, Astrid thrust three fingers into Sora's cunt, prompting Sora to arch up onto her toes before sinking, trembling, down onto them. Slowly, with all the force her sinewy arm could muster, Astrid pulled out, and then thrust back in —deeper, harder. And again. Sora's juices dripped down Astrid's fingers, seeping onto her palm, down her wrist. Then those fingers curled, hooking onto Sora's pubic ridge inside and dragging her toward Astrid's face.

Astrid inhaled deeply, then blew out against Sora's exposed, swollen flesh. Then Astrid released her, withdrawing her slick hand.

"Do you miss me?" she asked.

"Hardly," sighed Sora.

Astrid looked up at her skeptically. "All right, then," she said. "Time for your test." She brought her own wrist to her lips, and dragged the flat of her tongue lazily up it, collecting the sticky juices until she sucked her fingers into her own mouth.

"Ugh," she spat, as she finished cleaning herself, "disgusting." Then she spread Sora's knees with her elbows, and dove in, all lips and tongue and teeth.

Sora cried out again at the unexpected invasion, then mastered her breathing sufficiently to demand, "If it's *disgusting*—why don't you—*stop?*"

Astrid growled into her pussy, lapping and pressing her tongue—her whole sharp, slender little jaw—as deeply as she could manage before pulling back enough to gasp, "I *am!*"

Sora huffed a laugh, grinding now against her mouth and groaning at the girl's eager feast. "Do it, you weak little egg," she urged, almost taunting. "Quit."

"I—" Astrid began, delving back in to suck hard on her clit one—two—three last times, before pulling back—

. . . And finding resistance? Something was pressing her face into Sora's pussy, so roughly she nearly panicked for need of air. It was—she flailed against it, pushing against Sora's thighs in desperation—Sora's *hands!* Loose, and *so* strong, gripping her scalp with brutal force.

Seeing Astrid's wild, panicked eyes, Sora yanked her hair back so Astrid gasped up at her, utterly bested. The astonishment on that beautiful, foxlike face gratified Sora to her core; it felt almost as good as the girl's tongue had. Possibly almost better? But why choose, when she could have both? Once Astrid had refilled her lungs, Sora wasted no time in reclaiming her face.

And gods, but the girl sucked with a new ferocity now. Sora clung to her, nails scraping raw against her scalp, her neck, as Astrid pressed her to the wall, eating her like her last meal, or like a wolf finally tearing into its first.

When Sora came, screaming her conquest and also her defeat, Astrid held on with her hands, white-knuckled, her teeth barely sheathed in her lips, until Sora sank, tremors overtaking her, to the floor. Astrid followed her down, panting and spent.

After a silent moment, Astrid felt fingers in her hair again. Stroking gently.

"You know I could have just disappeared," Astrid rasped, her throat raw.

Sora chuckled. "Then why didn't you?"

Astrid paused for a long moment, thinking. "I didn't want to," she finally answered, smothering the confession with defiance.

Sora nodded. Clearly, she understood.

"How'd you do it?" Astrid asked her. "When did you get loose?"

Sora chuckled. "As if I'd tell you for free."

Astrid raised an eyebrow. "What would it cost me?"

Sora raked her gaze over her pointedly, not missing her sodden panties, messily askew. "Possibly some . . . 'soup.'"

Acknowledgments

Our fervent thanks go out to our faithful Patreon subscribers, who have given us the audience and support to write and produce these stories each month. You've made a dream possible! We have loved meeting so many of you through your thoughtful comments and over video chat dates; the presence of this community means the world to us.

Especial thanks to patrons: Kris M., Everleigh E., JK Barbarian, Katie Keith, Cari Aida, Kat Harrell, Sam Bahr, Michelle V., Kieran the Barbarian, Jeem | Nightworldlove, Carrie Moore, Samantha Bourbon, Socheata Chan, Catie Dale, Vesper Doom, Jen Graham, Mark Ring, Veronica Duff, Heather Lo & Diana Perry, Nicole Lafrenière, Angelo Comeaux, Michelle Clark, Carrie Ellison, Lynette Sullivan, Angel T., Star Robinson, Lori Lynn Tucker, Kayleigh Littler, Kaitlyn M., Patience Tuesday, Stacey Kruml, Jo Blackthorn, Mari L., Saoirse Burleson (First of his name), Darren Hennessey, Linnea, Ezri Legler, Ludmilla Suzan, Malea Thomas, Jennifer Nerdahl, Annie Lechak, Aaron Pants, Freyja Brandel-Tanis, and Tae Malin!

We also could not possibly have done this without our wonderful cover artist, Nienke Slotboom. We were hoping for so many tricky qualities in a cover: we wanted to be age, race, and body type unspecific, but to still portray two women. We wanted to convey unmistakably that this book is comprised of NSFW content, but with imagery that's comfortable (and enjoyable!) to promote. We wanted sparks, and something with feeling. It was so much to ask, and Nienke delivered *so beautifully*, we still can't believe how much we love her work.

Thank you to Emily Colin, whose conceptual consult was so generous and helpful!

Huge thanks to Jamie and Crystal, our lovely beta readers —and to Michelle and Laura, who both donated so much time and attention to our copy edit! You've improved this immeasurably with your steadfast efforts to see past the steamiest stuff in our brains in order to address those extraneous semicolons. Thank you both for all your priceless advice about every detail along the way. And of course, eternal gratitude to Michelle for first inspiring the yarn meet cute in Michaels, even if she was too straight to fully appreciate that bit of sapphic perfection playing out in her real life.

Thank you to Don, for your support and everything else: we love you. Finally, thank you to our delightful children, who were all duly scandalized on seeing the cover of their moms' first cowritten book.

About the Authors

"A fave among audiobook listeners" (Buzzfeed), **Natalie Naudus** is one of the most beloved audiobook narrators working today. She has won a dozen Earphones awards, including one for her own debut novel, *Gay the Pray Away*. She has degrees in vocal performance from George Mason University and the University of North Texas. Her hobbies include crocheting, gardening, and attending all her daughters' hockey games. Find her on Instagram, TikTok, Audible, Libro.fm, Quinn, and www.natalienaudus.com.

Mary Helen Gallucci is an audiobook narrator and editor, dabbling also in Foley effects for Natalie's audio productions on the Quinn platform. A former violin, literature, and drama teacher, she has degrees in music and medieval literature from Northwestern University, Western Michigan University, and the University of Notre Dame. Her hobbies include making stained glass art, playing a variety of instruments, and going to therapy/reading self-help books to be a cycle-breaking mother. Find her on Audible, Libro.fm, and www.maryhelen gallucci.com.

Find Us Online!

Natalie's debut novel, *Gay the Pray Away*, is available in print, e-book, and audiobook (narrated herself) anywhere books are sold. It's hot to shop indie!

Sapphic Sparks is also available as an audiobook, narrated by the authors.

To hear more "Sparks" monthly, subscribe to our our Patreon! And keep an eye out for *Sapphic Sparks* volume 2, coming June 2026.

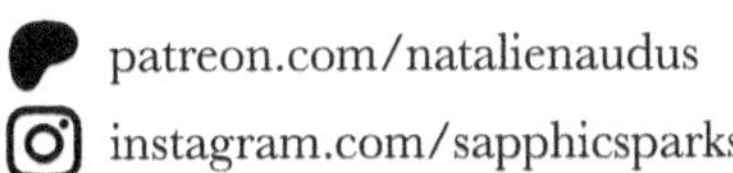

patreon.com/natalienaudus

instagram.com/sapphicsparks